This is a work of fiction. Name
events, and incidents are either
Imagination or used in a fictiti
to actual persons, living or de..,
coincidental.
Copyright © 2019 JB Trepagnier
All Rights Reserved. No part of this publication may be
reproduced, stored in a retrieval system, or transmitted, in any
form or any means – by electronic, mechanical, photocopying,
recording, or otherwise without prior written permission

2

My Cat is The AntiChrist

JB Trepagnier

Table of Contents

Chapter 1 5
Chapter 2 9
Chapter 3 12
Chapter 4 18
Chapter 5 26
Chapter 6 34
Chapter 7 40
Chapter 8 47
Chapter 9 50
Chapter 10 55
Chapter 11 58
Chapter 12 63
Chapter 14 68
Chapter 15 74
Chapter 16 81
Chapter 17 85
Chapter 18 90
Chapter 19 102
Chapter 20 110
Chapter 21 120
Chapter 22 125
Chapter 23 128
Chapter 24 136
Chapter 25 142
Chapter 26 146
Chapter 27 151
Chapter 28 156
Chapter 29 159
Chapter 30 161

Chapter 31 169
Chapter 32 173
Chapter 33 177
Chapter 34 181
Chapter 35 185
Chapter 36 189
Chapter 37 193

Chapter 1

Someone was trying really hard to disturb my slumber. I wondered which group was trying to save my soul this time. I'd disabled the damned doorbell because they just flocked to me. It'd been that way since I was a kid in the foster system. They were all perfectly nice. They were never mean, even when I got older, dyed my hair purple, pierced several body parts, and started wearing black lipstick. It was really weird. It didn't matter if they were Jehovah's Witnesses or Southern Baptist, they all seemed really concerned about some epic mistake I was going to make.

I was twenty-six now, and it was probably way too late for whatever mistake they were worried about, but they kept knocking on my door at ass o'thirty in the morning talking about this mysterious mistake. Between my dating history, ruining any chances at college, and hell, my history at killing plants, that mistake was probably long gone.

I was a bartender and kept late hours, so people knocking on my door that didn't have a pizza in their hands weren't welcome. I'd put all sorts of signs with profanity about disturbing me all over my door, and a *beware of people eating dog* sign. Most people who tried to knock this early gave up when I didn't drag myself out of bed to answer, but whoever was out there was a persistent little shit.

I decided to traumatize whoever it was. I wasn't shy about my body. For a time, I'd bartended at a strip club where I might as well have been naked. The air conditioner in my apartment was worthless, so I was in bed surrounded by fans and no clothes. Whoever was at my door was getting a little show.

I heaved myself out of bed and stalked to the front door wearing nothing but my tattoos. I threw the door open expecting to scare off some old church ladies. Instead, there was a man in a suit that looked like it cost an entire year of rent and my nakedness didn't seem to faze him.

He just peered at me over the rim of his glasses. "Tabitha? Why don't you put some clothes on so we can talk?"

That was a first. He wasn't even looking at my boobs. He was looking me right in the eye, and his gaze never strayed. Now, I was actually feeling self-conscious about standing in my doorway ass naked.

"How do you know my name?" I demanded. "And who are you?"

"I'm the attorney handling the estate for your parents. Your *birth* parents. We thought they died without an heir or a will. I found a lot of photos of you in a locked drawer in your father's desk. He'd paid someone to watch you for your entire life."

I felt the bottom fall out of my stomach. I never knew anything about my birth parents and my time in the foster system had been awful. All I knew was that I'd been dumped somewhere when I was two. I was never formally adopted, and most of my foster parents had like, twenty other foster kids collecting checks while we all slept on air mattresses on the floor.

"I'm not sure I care," I snapped, crossing my arms. "If he had someone watching me, then he knew how hard I grew up and never tried to rescue me."

"Miss? Do you think you could put some clothes on so we can chat? You've inherited a rather large estate and sum of money. You can be mad at them all you want, but that house is surely a better place to live than here," he said, eyeing my piece of shit apartment.

I bit my lip. I wanted to be mad, but some people had closets bigger than my apartment and shit was always breaking. If I asked my landlord to fix something, he thought I'd fuck him for repairs, and I ended up on YouTube trying to fix it myself. A house I didn't have to pay for and an inheritance to keep me comfortable for a little while could give me a needed break from having to pretend to flirt with drunk men so they would give me a decent tip.

"What's your name, anyway?" I asked, stepping away from the door to let him in.

"I'd much prefer to have this conversation with you clothed. You may call me Mattan. Just Mattan will do. It's what everyone calls me."

"Well, Mattan, make yourself as comfortable as you can on that shitty couch while I put clothes on."

I already knew Mattan's ass was going to hurt as soon as he sat down on that couch. I'd been living in this shit hole since I got out the foster system and some of the furniture, I found on the side of the road. That couch was from dumpster diving, and it didn't matter where you sat, you were going to get a spring up your ass.

Since I was talking to him about my future, it didn't seem right to do it in sweatpants and a tank top, but the rest of my clothes were for going out or work. I just shrugged. If my father kept photos of me in some big secret locked desk, then he'd probably already seen me in leather pants and a corset. I didn't bother with the corset because I was thinking about his ass on my couch and just put on a sheer top.

When I got back to the living room, Mattan was shifting uncomfortably on my shit-brown couch. I sat on the other end. I was used to the damned thing and didn't even react to the spring in my ass.

Mattan saw right through the bold look I was giving him.

"You want to know why you were given up, but he had someone watch you."

I hid my expression. "Well, since you didn't know I existed, I'm guessing that answer died with him."

"Actually, no. I think I have an answer. Your parents were important people in certain circles. Some would say dangerous circles. I found a record of another child, your brother. I found his baby photos, then nothing else. It was like he totally disappeared. There is a very good chance you ended up in foster care, and he watched you for your safety."

"So, you're telling me this big offer of yours puts me in danger?" I knew it was too good to be true.

"I don't think so. Their manor house is basically like a huge fortress."

He was bull shitting me. There was something he wasn't telling me. "I'm twenty-six, so my parents can't have died from old age. Fortress or not something got to them."

"The stairs got to them. They were having a dinner party. Your parents liked to entertain, and they always made a huge entrance. The manor has this huge staircase. They were announced and were posed at the top of the stairs arm in arm. One of them tripped and took the other with them. They both broke their necks in the fall."

"Can I bring my roommate to live with me?"

Mattan looked around my tiny apartment like he had no idea how there was another bedroom in here. But he surprised me. He'd clearly done his research on me before he got here.

"Elizabeth. You call her Lizzie. You grew up in foster care together. She's not here now?"

"Lizzie is with her girlfriend. She's totally in love with her, but I think her girlfriend is just dragging her along. She can do so much better," I sniffed.

Mattan appeared to be unflappable. "Once all the paperwork is signed, the manor is yours, and you can have whom you like live there. I traveled a long way to find you, and I'd hate to go back without you."

"Where is this mysterious manor?"

Mattan grinned at me. "Salem. A long ways away, but if you can gather your things and Lizzie, I've got a private jet waiting to take you there."

Just last night, I'd gotten shorted on tips for nearly breaking the hand of a man who decided to grab my ass. His friends held it against me too, and I left the bar with shit money wondering how I was going to make rent. I wondered what kind of karma I invoked to have Mattan end up on my doorstep and not get offended at my greeting to actually tell me about my inheritance.

Maybe there were answers about my past and how I ended up in foster care in that secret drawer of photos of me.

CHAPTER 2

Mattan left me to pack and try to convince Lizzie to come with me. I pretty much intended to leave everything behind except my wardrobe. I had no sentimental tokens of my past, but I did have some kick-ass clothes. I already knew when Lizzie would be home. Her girlfriend kicked her out her apartment without breakfast so she could get ready for work. That was just another reason I didn't like her. If you really loved someone, you at least fed them before you booted them out your bed.

Lizzie came home as I was throwing clothes in bags. She worked at the same bar I did and kept late hours. She heard me moving around and stuck her head in my bedroom door.

"What the fuck are you doing awake, Tabitha? You never move before noon."

"You're never going to believe this shit, Lizzie. You're going to need to sit down."

Lizzie eyed my bags of clothes. We ended up in the same foster home when I was fourteen and Lizzie was sixteen. She aged out before I did. As soon as I was out, we moved in together. Lizzie wasn't my blood, but she would always be my sister, and she knew damned well I wasn't going anywhere without her. She took a running start a dove into my bed. The frame was a dumpster dive, but the mattress and box spring were paid for with saved tips. My bed and Lizzie's bed were probably the only comfortable things in the house.

"There was a man at the door before you got home—"

"We have to move because you have a stalker from the bar? Shit, Tabby, why don't we just scare the shit out of him like the last one?"

"No, a lawyer. About my birth parents and some inheritance. If I sign some shit, I get a house and some money. We could just chill for a little while depending on how much money it is. If it's a lot, we could build that club we always talked about. We'd be our own bosses for once."

"What's the catch? There's always a catch with us."

"We'd have to move to Salem, but shit, Lizzie, he's going to bring us there in a private jet."

Lizzie snorted, then stretched on my bed like a cat. "If they're still burning people as witches, we wouldn't last two minutes there."

I threw a pair of sweatpants at Lizzie. Between the two of us, my hair was purple and hers was blue. We were probably equal in the number of piercings and tattoos we both had. I favored leather and corsets, and Lizzie was a Lolita through and through. Neither of us gave two shits about what people thought when we went out, and we were both giggling at the idea of what new neighbors would think. We found some people's reactions to us when they saw us for the first time hilarious, especially when they tried to hide their children.

"I doubt it. Mattan would have said something, and he didn't react at all when I answered the door naked."

Lizzie cocked her perfectly sculpted eyebrow at me. "He didn't even check out your tits? Is he a zombie?"

"He kept calling the house a manor, and he's going to bring us there in a private jet. There probably is some huge catch, but doesn't it sound like it's worth it just to get out of here and finally not be broke?"

Lizzie just shrugged. "You know I'd follow your ass anywhere. I didn't even ask you how you felt about finding out about your birth parents. You always swore you didn't want to know."

"I'm curious now. I wasn't a baby when I ended up in foster care, but Mattan didn't know about me. My parents were in Salem, but they paid someone here to follow me and take photos. I want to know how they hid a baby when he said they were famous for their parties and why they watched me for so long, but never did anything. Whatever Mattan's catch is, those answers are in Salem in their house."

Lizzie hopped out of my bed and hugged me. I didn't need to go into some wordy explanation. Lizzie and I had always understood each other. That was why we always promised to stay together.

"When do we leave? I'll start packing."

That was my girl. Mattan told me he would be on standby waiting for my call. I knew Lizzie would be ready to get out of here with just her clothes just as much as I was. Mattan just had this face you could trust. If there were a catch, he would have told me if it was horrible.

Chapter 3

Mattan actually sent a fucking limousine to pick us up when I called. Neither of us had a license and hadn't bothered to learn to drive because we knew it would be a cold day in hell before we could afford a car. We took the bus until we both had enough tips to buy a simple bike and just rode it everywhere. It was a bitch to bring more than a few bags of groceries home, but it kept my thighs in excellent shape.

It was one of those stretch SUV limousines that easily fit all our bags. Lizzie and I were acting like total idiots, bouncing on the seats and rolling the windows down to wave at people like we were the Queen of England. There was even a small refrigerator with champagne in the fucking thing. It was the good stuff too. Lizzie and I had cheap champagne at parties, but it was like sharp, carbonated water. I thought champagne was horrible until I drank it out the back of an SUV.

Lizzie and I were buzzed when we got to the runway. Mattan didn't even comment as we giggled and stumbled all over the place like idiots. He nodded his head and men started unloading our bags to put in the plane.

"The food on the plane is excellent. We should get ready to board."

That was the only comment he made on our drunkenness. I knew he wanted us to eat to sober up. As soon as he mentioned food, my stomach turned in on itself. Aside from the occasional pizza delivery and if I got free pub food at work because someone sent an order back to the kitchen, Lizzie and I ate cheap food from boxes that you nuked in the microwave. We were both probably radioactive at this point if that was a thing.

Neither of us had eaten. The idea of getting out of Podunk Kentucky and the promise of money had us packing in a whirlwind. I made a quick stop at the apartment office and promised not to make a stink about my deposit if my landlord hauled the furniture out. I saw his small, beady eyes plotting. I already knew what he was going to do. He was going to leave our furniture there, jack up the rent, and advertise it as a furnished apartment because he was a greedy little shit.

I'd never been on a plane before, much less a private jet. The seats were comfortable, and my head started nodding as soon as I rested into the cushions. I realized how tired I was. I answered the door naked early this morning, and now I was on a plane to a new state and a new house. I couldn't sleep. I needed answers, and I might as well ask while Mattan was stuck in a plane and had nowhere to go.

"Is there a coffee machine on this thing?" I asked.

I'd hardly gotten the word coffee out, and there was a man at my armrest asking me what kind of coffee I preferred. Lizzie and I had a coffee machine, and we drank our coffee straight black, like our souls. I just wanted caffeine, but I got to be fancy today. Lizzie had already ordered some Mocha Latte abomination with caramel and whipped cream. I needed black fuel, so I just said I wanted espresso.

Mattan was giving us both this look like this kindly, grandfather figure. "You can take a nap, you know. I realize I was very early this morning."

The dude who took our coffee order was snappy. He had our coffee and some sort of flaky pastries on a tray before I could even start firing questions at Mattan. Maybe that was his big plan. Fling caffeine and sugar at me so I wouldn't ask. I'm not going to lie; it was totally a trick that would work on me. I worked in a coffee shop in high school, and this wasn't a pastry we served. It was beautiful, and it smelled better than any Danish I threw at college students trying to study.

"*Paris-Brest* is my favorite," Mattan said. "I had the chef at the Rothledge Manor make it if I could convince you to come back.

You'll find the staff there quite welcoming and willing to cook whatever you desire."

Lizzie was already inhaling that pastry and nearly choked. "The fucking house has a name? Every house with a name I've heard of has poltergeists, Casper the friendly ghost, or dead bodies in the walls."

Whatever, I was waiting for Mattan to answer because I'd seen the same horror movies Lizzie had. I didn't want to start some sort of renovations and get introduced to the corpse of some great uncle in my new walls. Houses with names or on some nefarious hill always had weird shit going on. Maybe that was the catch.

Mattan must have been a saint. Lizzie practically barfed that pastry everywhere when she found out our new home had a name and I'm pretty sure some of it got on him. He was just giving us this serene look like he didn't think we were a bunch of savages.

"Well, there *is* a family graveyard in the back plot, but the house is perfectly normal. Tabitha, your family, the Rothledges and the Lambs were originally from the Holy Land with different names, of course. The legend is that the Rothledges, the Lambs, and many of the original families in Salem were part of the same tribe. They fled the Holy Land together and settled in Europe, only to have to flee again for intolerance, even if they hid their faith.

"They thought they would find tolerance and peace in the New World, then the Salem Witch trials happened. All of the families were quite wealthy and with standing in the community, but at that time, speaking against something like that would just have you burned with the rest of them. The original families do have their own lore and superstitions, mainly about the Lambs and the Rothledges and I suspect that was how no one knew about you, Tabitha."

That pastry felt like a rock in my throat. If he was about to tell me that my hellish childhood and secret births were because my parents and all these families still believed in the boogeyman, he was going to wear this fucking pastry.

"Is Tabby going to be in danger from them if we go back?" Lizzie demanded. "I *knew* this was too good to be true."

"Both of you, no," Mattan said gently. "*I'm* part of the original families, and I mean Tabitha no harm. The rest of the families don't either. I've already asked. Tabitha raises a lot of questions we *all* want answers to. We think your parents, Elliot and Levana, had the answers, but they can't tell us."

"Can't tell you what?" I shrieked. Mattan was about to have a pastry in his face, and then I was going to barge in the cockpit and demand someone turn this plane around.

"It's probably nothing, but your parents obviously believed it. Twenty-six years ago, they stopped throwing parties and sort of secluded themselves for about two years. That would have been when Levana was pregnant with you and until you were two years old. Something happened that you ended up in foster care in Kentucky instead of being raised with all of us. We all want that answer. The families are still close."

"Mattan, if you don't stop giving me half answers, I swear to god I'm going to shove this coffee mug up your ass," I snapped.

"Sorry, Tabitha, it's just that you've been away for so long and there's a lot to fill in. From what we've always been told and has been passed down through generations is that a Rothledge and a Lamb shouldn't mix. All we knew is that in the past, bad things happened when they did. We all thought it was silly superstition when your mother and father fell in love. Most everyone, aside from older generations, was happy for them and threw a huge wedding. The families your parent's age wants to know how you ended up in Kentucky just as much as you and Lizzie. We've petitioned the elders for answers."

I had my coffee, and that huge revelation certainly woke me up. Now, I wished I had just taken a nap and waited for answers. Who still had elders around? Mattan must have noticed my head was swirling. He snapped his fingers, and the kid who took our coffee order was back.

"Something a bit stronger. The vintage from twenty-six-years ago now that we know why it was released."

I had a feeling whatever that kid was going to bring out wasn't cheap beer or vodka. Hell, it probably had gold flakes in it or some shit. An hour on a private jet and I was already turning into a pretentious ass.

"Who's the kid you're bossing around?" I asked. I always found out the names of people waiting on me. I tried to tip well and be kind to them.

"My nephew, doing a little punishment and learning the family business. You can call him Benjy like everyone else. My family made their fortune in coffee. It's sold all over the world, and we have a few coffee shops around Salem. The coffee shops are new, but once the kids in the family are old enough, they spend a few years working as baristas for inspiration. Benjy decided to keep bothering a female patron after she told him no several times, so Benjy gets to fetch things for a little while until he learns no means no."

I cocked an eyebrow at Mattan. I liked his family. They could do a number on several of the men I served drinks to. Benjy wasn't even complaining about waiting on us. I had no idea he was Mattan's relative at all. I was going to try to get to know Benjy when he came back, but my mouth fell open when he handed a bottle to his uncle. I had no idea what was in it, but the bottle had jewels in the glass, and just the empty bottle would have paid my rent for over a year.

Mattan seemed like he was trying to relax me after that bomb he just dropped on me. "The Rothledges are distillers. Maybe you've heard of them? They've gotten so famous, their blends are coveted in certain circles, and new releases are celebrated. Sometimes, one generation might only release one new vintage because coming up with the blend and letting it age takes so long.

"When your parents' sort of went into their seclusion twenty-six-years ago, fifty bottles of this were released. The families all get one as we share everything. That's why I had this and brought it with me. I wouldn't normally open one of your family's blends unless it was a really special occasion, but I think finding you counts."

Lizzie had this horrible habit of snorting when she found something funny. "Well, we definitely know he's not lying about finding your real parents. You've always had a knack for pairing booze and mixing drinks."

"And now you don't have to do it for meager tips for awful men," Mattan pointed out, pouring drinks. "For this particular blend, your parents broke out a barrel of single malt whiskey aged for sixty-five years in a sherry-infused cask and another oak barrel aged seventy-years. I know it was to celebrate your birth, it's just as well I open it with you."

The whiskey we served at the bar was probably nowhere near as potent as what was being poured in that glass. All I'd eaten was that pastry. I apparently came from a family with a lot of history, and I didn't need to be getting totally shit faced. I had a high metabolism and a stomach like a bottomless pit after growing up never having enough to eat.

"You said the food on the plane was good?" I asked.

Mattan handed out goblets and snapped his fingers. Once again, Benjy came back without complaint. We weren't asked what we wanted. Mattan just told him to bring the food out. I hated going on a first date with someone, and they thought they could order for me. They never got a second date. Mattan saw the look I was giving him.

"We had to prepare the food and bring it on the plane. There's not a kitchen here. I had the chefs at your parent's house prepare their favorite meal. I know you don't remember them, but all of us will share our memories with you, and we'll figure out together what happened to you. I have lobster rolls and poached pears."

Pears were always my favorite when my foster families could afford them. And I'd always wanted to try lobster. So did Lizzie. We were always in sync, even at fifteen. I was starting to wonder if there was more to Mattan and my family history than he was telling me. He seemed to know everything we would want.

Maybe there was a catch. Maybe I was making a deal with the devil.

CHAPTER 4

I finally passed out after I ate all that delicious food. I didn't get more answers from Mattan about my past. The last thing I remembered was Benjy taking my plate and just wanting to rest my eyes for a few minutes. I finally woke up again when we landed, and Lizzie was shaking me. There was another huge car waiting for us to take us to my new house.

Mattan pointed up ahead at my new house. I saw a large gate and a huge manor house up on a hill.

"Holy fuck, a name, and a hill. There's definitely dead bodies or some fucked up shit going on in that house," Lizzie said, looking over my shoulder.

The house was huge and old, but it wasn't scary looking. It looked like it had been well cared for, despite being old. It looked like some old castle with spires and turrets. I half expected a moat when the gate swung open, and the car drove through it. The driveway was well maintained, and there were no bumps, even if it was curvy.

Mattan looked like he was hiding something. Benjy was with us and bouncing in his seat. I thought I would be given a tour and would sign some papers to make everything mine. I was shocked when Mattan threw open the door, and we walked into this foyer with twenty-foot ceilings and a huge chandelier that it was full of people. There were streamers, and it sounded like someone was playing the fucking kazoo.

"Surprise!" everyone yelled. I noticed the *Welcome Home, Tabitha* sign draped across the ceiling.

I remembered every horror movie I'd ever seen and what Lizzie's theories were. I leaned in and clutched her arm. "Think they are going to eat us?" I whispered. "Fuck!" I yelled, practically climbing the wallpaper.

Something brushed against my shins. When I looked down, it was even worse. It looked like someone mixed a bat and a feline. The thing had no hair, huge ears like it could take flight, big green eyes, and it was wearing a fucking sweater. Lizzie wasn't alarmed by the bat-rat-lizard-cat thing in the sweater. She leaned down and held out her hand for it to sniff like I didn't just warn her someone here might eat us.

Mattan rushed forward and scooped the weird hairless thing up. It let out a raspy meow, and its eyes never left me as Mattan scratched his head. "Someone couldn't put Drake away for the surprise party?"

"You know he bites everyone that isn't family," a woman called. "You should warn Tabitha now that infernal cat is a full-time job."

It was like the cat could hear her and hissed at her. Mattan just made cooing noises and scratched his chin. "There, there. Don't let the horrid lady bother you. I'll put Drake in his bedroom while all of you get to know Tabby and Lizzie."

The cat had his own bedroom? I got sent to foster care, but this mutant cat had his own bedroom and a warm sweater? The woman who spoke must have been able to tell I was about to have a meltdown. She was dressed like a really rich hippy, in a flowing gown with jewels dripping from her ears and wrists.

"Let's forget about that horrid cat," she said, weaving her arms through me and Lizzie's. "My name is Odelia, and we are all *very* excited to have you here. If my daughter ever shows her face, she's going to want to know what dye you use in your hair. She's been trying for purple for years, and she always ends up with lavender. Ariel is a Gothic Lolita like Lizzie here, and I imagine you'll have so much fun sharing clothes."

Odelia was shorter than both me and Lizzie, but we were also wearing high heeled fuck me boots. Lizzie shot me this look over her head, and I already knew what it meant. Neither of us knew if this was real. I didn't know if I was dreaming and was going to wake up any minute or I really had ended up in this strange world where my parent's friends had children my age like me.

Another woman who was dressed like she came straight out of Victorian England blocked our path. Her red curls were piled on her head, and she had this pinched face. I thought she was going to be totally nasty to all three of us, but she just gave Odelia this chastising look like they were old friends.

"Really, Odelia. We both know our wayward children aren't coming here. If they had known they had so much in common with Tabitha and Lizzie, they still wouldn't have come because they thought we were lying to them to get them to another boring party. You realize what this means, don't you?"

I certainly didn't. This knowing look passed between them like this big secret was shared, then it passed just as quickly as I saw it. They both broke into huge smiles, and I already knew they were hiding something.

"Tabitha, Lizzie," the red-haired woman said, giving us a curt nod. "My name is Esther. My daughter, Natalia, dresses like Tabitha. We know we are all your parent's age and you'd probably prefer to be with people your own age. So, I'm going to use a term from your generation. We're going to have to take a selfie with you and send it to Ariel and Natalia to get them here."

"Can we wait? There are so many people here, and I'm already going to have trouble keeping everyone straight. I can meet everyone's kids later. Mattan kind of just woke me up and I hopped on a plane and came here. I'm still not even sure this is real. That thing in the sweater has me wondering if this is a nightmare."

Esther snapped her fingers. "Emergency provisions. We have a crisis. Tell me, girls, are you more of a whiskey or rum type of person and when you are to eat your feelings do you go for sweet or savory?"

"Well, before we got on that plane, we were dead ass broke. Getting over a crisis involved a cheap bottle of vodka and a fun-sized bag of M&M's," I pointed out.

Odelia just grinned and nodded to Esther. "Take them to Elliot and Levana's sanctuary, and I'll handle provisions."

I took Esther for being a little stuffy, but she looked practically impish when she leaned in and told us to be as quiet as possible as we disappeared because the rest of the group there was a bit stuck up. She led us through a maze of hallways and a hidden door. The door was actually built into the wood paneling in the wall. I was starting to wonder what the hell I'd gotten myself into again. Secret rooms and rooms just for bat cats?

I looked around. This was my first secret room, after all. I should at least see what people chose to do when they were paranoid and had so much money, they built these things. It was so…not what I was expecting. I guess I was expecting maps with pinpoints on the wall, televisions screens all showing Alex Jones or some other nutty conspiracy nut, and news clippings about aliens or bigfoot.

There was no television in here at all. There were plush couches and chairs and what looked like surround sound speakers. It looked like they did craft projects in here. I could see where someone was working on carving wooden chess pieces, and someone else was knitting a sweater. It looked like it was for that cat with the bat ears. That just set me off again. I grew up in ill-fitting clothes that were handed down to me.

Esther clearly saw right through me. She led Lizzie and me over to the sofa. "Odelia and I were like you and Lizzie with Levana. I had the same reaction you did when I saw the cat. He's apparently a Russian breed called a Peterbald. They crossed an Oriental Shorthair with a hairless Russian breed. Did you know Drake has webbed feet and can open doors? Your mother had to bathe him once a month because of his skin, and he needed sweaters in the winter because of drafts in this house. Most of us have cats. It's just a thing with the families.

"It's like Drake never ages. He should be slowing down since he's so old. No one but Levana and Elliot has ever been able to get his sweaters on him or give him his baths. They tried having a maid do it, and then they tried having several groomers come in. Drake was just too much for all of them. Drake is on several lists for groomers if they see his name, they won't come out. If you can believe this, Drake made such an impression on everyone that came out, groomers were warning other groomers. After the Lambs died, the only person he'd let near him was

Mattan, which is curious. He took to Mattan right away, which is odd because something happened your parents would never tell us about that they didn't get along with Mattan very well."

"Am I in danger from Mattan? He seemed so nice. If he did something so horrible, my mother wouldn't tell her best friends, can I trust him?"

"You mother? Mattan just told us you were an heir," Esther said, raising an eyebrow.

Shit. Was I not supposed to say something because of that stupid urban legend?

Odelia came in the room followed by someone holding a tray. Odelia was scowling at Esther. "Mattan probably just filed their taxes past the deadline or messed up their money. Mattan is way too boring for a proper scandal. Why are you breaking all that out now and overwhelming Tabitha? I came armed."

A tray was set in front of me, and my inner bartender kicked in. "A Mudslide, Chocolate Cake shots, and I believe there's a Chocolate Mint Julep on here?"

Odelia grinned. "Well, you're definitely a Rothledge. Your mother's secret truffle stash should be…right in this drawer," she said, triumphantly pulling a golden box out a drawer. "The chef here also makes a mean steak, so that will be brought in when it's done. I made those drinks, so try not to give me a hard time if they aren't up to standard. I learned from your mother, but my family works in finance."

She seemed just to accept I was Levana's daughter without question. Esther seemed to as well. They were both looking at me with tears in their eyes.

"Mattan kind of explained to me the families and the tribes, but not in huge detail. I know there was some urban legend about some families never mixing. How many families are there?"

"The original families have always been thirteen. The stories about the Rothledges and the Lambs were kept with an elder, our historian. During the Salem Witch Trials, she was accused. She knew it was coming and sent her children away. Back then, there was no way to fight an accusation. Any way they tested you was going to kill you. From what's been passed down, they raided her house, and all of our histories should have been safe in a room very much like this one.

"The story goes that the families sent coded messages in ancient Hebrew. They founded a coded note and just assumed the symbols were witchcraft. They burned the manor with the elder locked inside it. They murdered her and took our history with it. Everyone has their own version of what was hidden in that house, but no one knows for sure."

Odelia claimed she couldn't mix drinks, but she would have made great tips at the seedy bar I worked at. I'd downed half the Mudslide, and between Lizzie and me, all the shots were gone. I had a good buzz going when someone came in with the trays with the steaks. Odelia didn't ask, but my steak was perfect. I could have put a Band-Aid on it and milked the cow.

Odelia and Mattan seemed to know what I liked without asking. Lizzie and I had the same Christmas tradition every year. We had no family except each other. We didn't keep ties with anyone else from the foster system. Every year, on Labor Day, we'd start putting tips into an old coffee can. Just small amounts we could spare. We'd pick up extra tips and work holidays like Halloween and Thanksgiving.

Christmas day, we'd take our coffee can to a steak restaurant open on Christmas day and splurge on real food. I preferred mine still mooing, and Lizzie liked to try to get us kicked out by ruining a perfectly good cow ordering it well done. I was looking at steaks cooked to perfection for how we ordered when we had our Christmas celebration.

I stopped cutting into my steak and looked at Odelia and Esther. "Okay, fess up. How did you know to tell the chef here steak *and* how to cook it for both of us? You can't say it was how my mother took hers because we've got no fucking idea who Lizzie's mother is!"

Esther was just grinning at me. "You'd make your parents so proud. Nothing gets past you. It's one of the theories among the families. We call it Intuition. Some think it's a form of magic. If you grew up here, your parents would have taught you. It's always helped us. If we need an answer to something, it just pops in our head. I wanted to know how I could make you happy and comfortable, and the answer just came to me," she shrugged.

"Are you telling me you're witches?" I asked.

Odelia just laughed. "That's certainly a theory. It's one of the dumber theories about the Rothledges and the Lambs. The child of a union between the two families was supposed to ignite some sort of magic the original tribes had. It's a stupid theory — something that's discussed at parties when people are drunk. It's a game to throw out theories as to what was in the old documents that got burned in that manor. Witches aren't real, Tabitha. Whatever superstition there was about your parents getting together was probably some old-world lore that's long been debunked."

Lizzie shoved a huge piece of steak in her mouth and started chewing like some goat. "Do you actually believe the shit coming out your mouth? Tabby's parents knew something that they hid her for two years. Then, something happened they sent her into a totally shit situation and replaced her with that fucking cat. Tabby and I never got our own bedrooms growing up. Apparently, her father sent someone to take photos of the shitty situation he put her in while the fucking cat got his own room, homemade clothes, and baths. Pretty much *none* of what we got in the foster system."

"Please, you have every right to be upset. Perhaps we need to explain the significance of the cat?" Odelia said. "We thought you and Drake were children they were thinking of adopting when we were going through their things. We found the photos of Tabitha, but we also found out she had a twin brother, Drake. *Something* happened to Drake. There are all these photos of you as children together, the photos of Tabitha as she grew up, then it was just like Drake ceased to exist. Whatever happened to Drake must have scared your parents into sending you away, but keeping an eye on you. The cat was a replacement for your twin, not you. I can show you all the files your parents kept on you. They were always watching over you."

I couldn't enjoy my bloody steak with all the theories running through my head. "If no one knew about us, then did they send me away because *I* hurt Drake?"

"Don't be fucking stupid, Tabby," Lizzie snapped. "Someone knew about the two of you. Even if they had a home birth and never went to a doctor, they would have had someone with medical training looking after your mother, especially with twins."

"Anyone of the thirteen families specialize in medicine?" I demanded. Lizzie was my soul sister because it was like we could complete each other's sentences. I would have had that same thought right after she did. Between the two of us, we would figure this out. If we didn't, I was getting the hell out of here. These people seemed nice, but they could be cannibal aliens for all I knew.

"No one that could deliver babies. The Beaumer's do medical equipment, but it's all cancer research. Danny and Miri don't even like children. Both their parents would be after them to continue their line, but they both have younger siblings that are married with children. Danny and Miri's siblings gave birth in a hospital, and both women wanted to be unconscious until it was over," Odelia said.

Esther snorted. "They both had the right idea. I insisted everything with Natalia was going to be this perfect, natural birth. I lasted about four hours before I wanted every drug available to me and a joint to ease the pain."

"*Someone* had to have helped them and known about me," I said, trying to redirect the conversation back to my situation.

Odelia just shook her head sadly. "All Mattan told us was that he found the heir to your parent's fortunes. We all thought you were a distant relative. Knowing your parents, they did everything themselves. We saw the photos, and we thought you and Drake were children your parents were thinking of adopting."

"So, no one knows anything," I groaned, slumping in my seat.

Esther came over to pat me on the back. "Your parents have the answers. And our ancestors built these manors with plenty of hiding places. Just because we haven't found the full answer *yet* doesn't mean we won't. Just enjoy your new home for now. We'll all help you in this quest."

Chapter 5

Rothledge Manor had to have at least thirty bedrooms, but after Esther and Odelia had gotten us sufficiently shitfaced and tried to show us around to pick a bedroom, Lizzie and I just picked the first bedroom we saw and crashed in bed together. This was probably just some spare bedroom, but the mattress had to be gel, and the sheets were softer than anything I'd slept on before.

Someone had to be waiting outside the door listening, and that creeped me out. As soon as they heard us moving, they knocked and asked us what we wanted for breakfast. They asked that like it wasn't noon and time for lunch. Even if it were noon, we both would have woken up and gone straight to the coffee machine and just mainlined black coffee until we were no longer hungry. We didn't have to do that anymore, but we also had no idea what to do with ourselves. We just burst into giggles and said to cook something special.

I wasn't thinking about my past or what happened to me before. I was just cutting up with Lizzie. It all came crashing back on me when that bald fucking cat managed to open the door and come swaggering into our bedroom. I knew he was named after my twin and he had to be ancient if he was still alive. He wouldn't have any grays since he had no hair, but he didn't seem to be slowing down in any way.

The cat seemed to be silently judging me as he walked around the room like we'd chosen the wrong bedroom or something. He was still wearing the same sweater from yesterday, and I knew no one in the house could change it without getting mauled. The cat and I just stared at each other from across the room. The cat looked like evil incarnate, but he was kind of cute with his big, bat ears and wrinkled skin.

"They said something about his skin getting irritated if he's not bathed. Do you think his sweater needs to be changed? He might be on some naughty list with veterinarians too," I said. I don't know why I was worried about the cat. Maybe because I now knew he wasn't replacing me, it had something to do with my twin.

Lizzie just shrugged. "I think that cat is the cutest thing I've ever seen. Do you think I could make us matching clothes?" she squealed. Lizzie had an ancient Singer sewing machine we found at Goodwill and made all her clothes. She was much better at sewing than I was.

It was like the cat understood and hissed at her. Lizzie just laughed. "Maybe he would prefer a cat-sized leather jacket like his sister?"

I swear, it was uncanny. As soon as Lizzie mentioned dressing the cat in leather, he started purring and rubbing against her legs. She crouched down and held out her fists, Drake gave her a few sniffs, then started rubbing his face against her hand. At least one of us could change his clothes, but I might have to bribe Lizzie to bathe the cat if I couldn't. The cat was an old man now. It was my job to take care of him in his twilight years. I wasn't a monster. That cat meant a lot to my parents, and even if I was still hurt they sent me away, I wasn't going to let a helpless animal suffer.

"Oh, Drake is soft! Come pet him, Tabby."

When I went to pet him, he bolted, but stopped at the door and was giving us this look. "I think he...wants us to follow him?" I said, shooting Lizzie a look. I was pretty sure I was going totally insane thinking the cat was trying to show me something. He was probably going to lead us to his food bowl. I just felt deep down in my bones it was important to follow that cat.

Drake led us down a long hallway. I knew I wasn't stupid. He'd run ahead, then stop and wait for us. He led us all the way down the hall to two ornate doors. Drake could open a door with those webbed feet if it were cracked just a little, but he couldn't reach these doorknobs. Lizzie and I just stood there and stared at the gilded doors.

"What do you think he's trying to show us?" I whispered.

Drake had sort of his hoarse, raspy meow and he just started wailing like he wanted us to hurry the hell up. I shrugged. Listening to a wailing, bald cat who wanted me to open a door wasn't the dumbest thing I'd done. I'd hardly spent any time with it, but I felt this odd kinship with that crazy cat. This cat was the closest thing left I had to my parents. It wasn't like he could tell me, but this cat knew secrets about my parents Esther and Odelia couldn't tell me.

I threw open the gilded doors. The suite was plush and ornate with a four-poster bed on a dais in the center of the room. This had to be my parent's suite. Did Drake have feelings and miss them too? I realized I didn't even know what my parents looked like. I talked to several of their friends, but I'd never seen photos. Drake ran to an archway off to the left. I curiously followed.

There was a sitting room with various games and hobbies my parents enjoyed, but Drake ran to the wall and stood under two portraits that had to be my parents. I was starting to wonder if Peterbald cats were also bred with some sort of evil cat genius and if I didn't watch Drake, he'd start planning world domination. I didn't need to be thinking about that. I was being stupid

The paintings were on the one bare wall in the room. I looked at my parents for the first time. If my hair hadn't been purple and my eyebrows less carefully tweezed, I'd be an exact replica of my mother. We were both fair-haired with delicate features. She looked like she was tall and small boned like I was. Her eyes were painted the same shade of blue as mine.

I looked over to my father's portrait. He was a handsome man, but I didn't look like I got anything from him. He had chestnut hair that brushed his collar. His eyes were so hazel they were almost amber. Where she was a delicate beauty, he was ruggedly handsome. I wondered what both of them were like and exactly what went on in this house that led up to my brother's disappearance and me being shipped off to Kentucky.

I didn't have time to think about it because Drake was howling again. Lizzie had come up and stood beside me.

"You think all this talk about witches and magic means Drake is really a familiar? I mean, he's pretty spritely for a twenty-four-year-old cat, and it seems like he's trying to communicate. Do you think you're really a witch, Tabby, and you can somehow talk to Drake?"

We didn't have cable, but we did have a shared Netflix account, and we both loved spooky shows. I wasn't shocked that was the first thing out of Lizzie's mouth after Drake brought us here, but it seemed like he was still trying to tell me something with all that wailing. I didn't want to entertain the notion of witches or familiars. I still wasn't convinced Drake didn't have some food bowl in here he wanted filling.

There were tables on either side of the paintings. Drake jumped on one of the tables and started pawing at the paneling on the wall. The idea that he might be some sort of familiar was starting to become more obvious as I remembered the secret room I got drunk in the night before. The door was activated by pressing on the paneling.

"Quick, Lizzie!" I said, running my fingers all over the wall. "I think there's another secret room in here."

Lizzie and I were both pressing on the walls like we weren't totally insane and following the instructions of a wailing cat. I felt something click under my finger and a small door opened up.

"Hah!" I yelled. "I'm not crazy!"

"No, this probably means you're a witch, you idiot."

"Well, the answers might be in that room."

Drake did all that wailing and running to get us to find this room, but he didn't seem to want us in there now. He blocked the small door and arched his back, hissing at us.

"Now what?" Lizzie asked. "Can you get rabies or cat cooties from a familiar?"

"Let's not test that theory. Remember the groomers? Let's not find out what happens when Drake is in a mood."

"Tabitha? Lizzie?" I heard someone calling our names.

Jana, the maid that asked us what we wanted for breakfast, stuck her head in. "I've been looking for you everywhere. Breakfast is ready, and you are both so thin. Will you come eat?"

Was Drake seriously blocking the door to the secret room because he knew breakfast was ready and wanted us to eat something? I looked at that cat suspiciously. He was sitting in the doorway giving himself a bath like a perfectly normal cat. Someone had better start answering questions because I certainly couldn't ask Drake.

"Should I bring the food in here or will you come down to eat?"

"If we come down, will you talk to us?"

Jana had to be in her sixties, so she must have been around when I was born. If my parents had locked themselves inside and weren't taking visitors, someone was bringing groceries and necessities to them. Maybe it was Jana or some of the other servants here.

"Of course. I know what questions you will ask, but I only have limited knowledge of what went on then. Your parents had us all sign so many nondisclosure agreements about talking about the children, but even if there's something in there about you, child, you deserve to know. Come down, and I'll answer what I know."

"Did you cook enough for you too?" I asked as I followed her downstairs.

"I ate before work. Come, you said fancy, so we went extra fancy to celebrate your arrival. Kosher Eggs Benedict and Hazelnut Crepes. I haven't made coffee because I'll need your input on that."

"Just black is fine," I said, ready to pepper her with questions. I was antsy as she set plates in front of me. I wanted to ask her questions, but I also wasn't used to being waited on. If I wanted food, I had to get up and make it or inhale it before it was gone.

Lizzie was still thinking about witches and familiars and asked Jana about that before I could ask anything.

"Strange things went on in this house, but I don't think witchcraft is involved. Drake has always been a peculiar cat, but have you ever owned a cat before? I have five at home. They used to be worshipped as Gods in certain points of history, and they certainly haven't forgotten that. Cats aren't like dogs who love you unconditionally. With cats, you have to earn it. Your parents had Drake shipped over from Russia for a lot of money. I think there's a part of Drake that just somehow knows your parents went through a lot of trouble to get him and just expects to be spoiled."

"How did no one know about me or my twin? Did my mother not have medical attention?"

"Ah, but she did. They had ultrasound machines and anything you could possibly find at a doctor's office shipped here. I have three daughters that chose to give birth at home. I was there helping for all of them. Your mother and father did a *lot* of research to do this on their own, and I was helping them. Drake came out first, and your father caught him. You came two minutes later, and I was the one you caught you because Drake was quite angry when he made his entrance in the world."

"Why were we hidden? What happened to Drake and why was I sent away?"

"I said I didn't have all the answers. Your parents went through a lot of trouble with the staff to keep you a secret. A lot of people were let go. Your parents only kept people they thought were trustworthy who wouldn't ask a lot of questions. We all knew we couldn't ask why the two of you needed to be kept a secret from everyone. From what I gathered, it was something only your mother and father knew, and they didn't want the other families to know."

"Did the secret get to be too much for them?"

"I honestly don't know what happened. You and Drake never had nannies, and we all had limited contact with you after you were born. After you were born and started getting older, something was happening that had your parents stressed and scared. No one came in the house, and no one knew about you. It was something that was happening behind closed doors, something that had to do with the big secret that had them scared.

"None of us knew what happened to either of you. It was like one day, the sound of toddlers was a normal thing in the house and the next day, it was gone. We never knew why a cat showed up a few days before the babies disappeared. Your parents were always kind to their servants. They paid us well and gave us plenty of time to be with our family. But this, whatever it was, it was something we knew if we asked, something bad would happen. Something very unlike your parents."

"Wait, I thought Drake the cat was bought after Drake my twin disappeared."

"A lot of people believe that and I'm probably one of the few people in the house who knows the truth. Drake the cat and Drake the boy were in the house at the same time, but very briefly."

"You don't think my parents *hurt* my twin, do you?"

"Not at all. Your parents loved both of you dearly, and I think you were told they threw a party as soon as you left. That wasn't the case. Levana and Elliot were in a dark place after the baby noise disappeared. It was a few months before they threw a party and I think that party was only to see if it could pull them out of a dark place. I worked all those parties, and I don't know how their friends never noticed their smiles never reached their eyes."

"Did you noticed anything weird going on in this house?"

Jana gave me a small, gentle smile. "You mean witchcraft? I'm sorry, I could help but overhear you and your friend. My family has worked for the Rothledges for ages. There were always a lot of secrets, but never anything that would send us running."

"That room Drake showed us, does everyone know about it?" Lizzie asked.

Jana sighed. "No, not even the servants know about all the secret rooms in this house. You parents rooms have always been off limits. They cleaned their chambers themselves, and I don't think they ever let their friends inside. When Mattan and everyone came here, they didn't know about you and Drake, but they seemed to know about most of the secret rooms. I know Mattan found the information about you in a room in your father's study."

"What do you want to do first, Tabby? The room in your parent's bedroom or the one in the study?" Lizzie asked.

"You should take that bedroom Drake showed you. It's yours by birthright and the master suite. The room you slept in last night was actually an old maid's quarter when maids used to live here. If you had gone one bedroom down, you would have seen it was adjoined to a better suite."

I don't think Jana meant to make Lizzie and I feel bad, but that "Maid's" room was bigger than our entire apartment back in Kentucky and furnished better than anything I'd ever owned before. Well, at least past the age of two when I was sent away. Maybe it would make me feel closer to my parents sleeping in their old bedroom. I had no idea. It depended on what I would find in their secret rooms first.

I thought whatever major secrets I would find would be in their bedroom, the room no one knew about. But I knew what everyone knew about me so far was in that room in his study. I needed to see those photos. Maybe my parents didn't know how bad it had gotten for me while I was in foster care and that was why they never came to get me.

There didn't seem to be any danger here, aside from weird cats who seemed to be able to show me things. I didn't *really* think he was some sort of familiar. If my parents had been witches, Jana's family would have seen something by now.

I didn't even need to tell Lizzie where we were going first. Jana started fussing as we both picked up our plates and tried to find a sink to wash them in. It was going to take a while before I got used to someone waiting on me. We ignored Drake's wailing and took Jana's directions to my father's study and how to open his secret room.

Chapter 6

Lizzie and I wandered down the hall trying to find the study. It was like the damned cat knew we were going there instead of the room he showed us. Drake was letting out these awful, hoarse wails and was intent on trying to trip us the entire walk there. We were clutching each other trying to stop the other from face planting when one of us was about to go down.

"Quit being a little shit, Drake," I fussed like he actually understood me. "I have time to explore that room."

That cat—he seriously hissed at me, and if he were capable of rolling his eyes at me, he would have. He let out that hiss and took a swipe at my legs, then sauntered off down the hall like he was totally done with us. I wondered if all cats were that weird or if it was just a Drake thing.

I knew we found the study because the doors were gilded like the bedroom doors. I wondered why all of the doors were unlocked. They had these locks on them that looked like it took a key from some old horror movie. My father's study looked like it was from some old movie. There were built in bookcases on every wall and a huge fireplace that had nymphs and satyrs carved into the mantle.

I was already told one of the grapes a satyr was holding would open a door next to the fireplace. I started running my fingers along the marble. Lizzie took the other side of the mantle.

"I get how Esther and Odelia knew about the room they took us to last night, but if Mattan had a falling out with my parents, how did *he* know about this room?" I asked. "I get all these family were close, but clearly, they kept secrets. How did Mattan know to look here? Don't you think it's weird out of all the safe rooms he could possibly find, he finds this one? We have hardly been here a day and we know about three. The cat showed us one of them, but it's weird."

"I didn't say anything because I wanted you to get answers about your family, but there's something about Mattan I don't trust. You said he didn't check out your tits at all and you were totally naked in front of him, but he was eye fucking me the entire plane ride because he liked my little outfit. Why me and not you? Every time we go out together, clueless dudes who don't understand Lolita culture and just Goth and can't tell us apart. We don't even have the same theme in tattoos. Mattan never checked you out once, but he was creeping me out."

"Lizzie, since when do you let someone creep on you without making them cry? We'll sign his papers, and then I can ban him from the house."

"Hah!" Lizzie yelled as one of the grapes she was fiddling with pressed in and a door started sliding open. "No, we need Mattan. We'll play the same game with Mattan we do when we're trying to get a big tip from a creeper who wants a quickie in the alley."

Mattan wasn't going to know what hit him any more than the unsuspecting idiots at the bar who liked to try to withhold tips for a blowjob. We'd get what we needed, and Mattan would be out on his ass. I already knew he did something to make my parents dislike him and *no one* creeped on my soul sister without consequences.

We walked through the door, and this secret room was totally different than the others. It was about the size of my bedroom back in Kentucky and looked like a research facility. There was a large wooden desk with what looked like a pretty high-tech computer on it. I was expecting file folders with photos if Mattan found info on me. I went straight to the desk drawer, and nothing was on paper. There were flash drives and nothing else.

I turned the computer on, and I already knew what I was going to see. A big *fuck you* box asking me for a password. Lizzie leaned over my shoulder.

"You remember that cute little hacker girl I dated? I'll bet the flash drives are encrypted too. You don't put data about a big secret child you don't want anyone to know about on anything electronic without locking it down like a fortress, even if it is in a secret room."

"Did the sexy hacker girl teach you anything?"

"Actually, several tricks, but nothing that would get us into this computer. The big question we need to be asking ourselves is how Mattan got in."

I shrieked and nearly threw the keyboard across the room when this hoarse sort of moan came from across the room. I thought it was the ghost of a corpse in the wall, and then I realized Drake had joined us again. He jumped on the desk and appeared to be strutting around like he was in some music video with male dancers in boy shorts.

I scratched him behind his ear since he was posing so hard to get our attention. "I sure do wish you could talk, Drake."

Drake started purring like the motor of a boat, and I swore it looked like he was smirking. I had no idea if he would bite me if I tried to grab him when he started walking on the keyboard. One of his webbed feet must have hit the *enter* key, and the computer booted right up. I just stared with my mouth wide open.

"No fucking way!" I yelled. "The cat knows the computer password and how to use a fucking computer? Lizzie, are you seeing this or am I going insane?"

"Well, that seals it, Tabby. You're a witch, and Drake is your familiar. It's the only thing that explains what we just saw. We need to start figuring out how to communicate with Drake because he has the answers you want."

"You want to start asking my parents friends how to talk to the cat when everyone we've talked to so far says we aren't witches. Do you think Drake unlocked the computer for Mattan too? Maybe my parents just trained Drake really well. If he was my family's familiar, why would he help Mattan?"

"Easy, stupid. To get you home. Maybe you have some big, cosmic destiny it's time for you to fulfill."

"I'm not a fucking Hobbit, Lizzie!"

"Well, I can't explain how the damned cat got you into the computer either. Let's just listen to that cat for now because he's the only one who seems to know anything. He wanted us in the bedroom, but he helped us get into the computer. Let's see what's here for now."

I started pulling flash drives out. They had dates written on them in marker. I started with the one that had my date of birth on it. I saw happy family videos of me and my twin. It was the first I was seeing of Drake. There were plenty of close-ups of the both of us. Even at only a few days old, Drake's eyes weren't blue like most babies. They were an inky black, and he had a thick head of black hair. His skin was pale white, and his cheeks didn't even get red when he had screaming fits. And he seemed to have a lot of those.

My parents seemed to be making a documentary about our lives or watching us for something. The cameras were almost always on us, and our parents commented on everything we did. It seemed like I was the calm to Drake's storms. When he was furiously screaming, nursing him or rocking him did nothing. Placing him next to me in the crib was the only thing that would get him to calm down. Once he was next to me, he would start cooing and sucking his fists.

My parents never said anything that had meaning to me or would give me an answer about what happened to Drake and me. I just got this vibe they were concerned about it from the tone of their voices. It was like they seemed to think it was something deeper than the twin bond I'd always read about.

Drake, the cat, hopped in Lizzie's lap and purred as he took a nap while we continued to pull out flash drives and watch videos. I watched Drake my twin, and I grow into toddlers. I grew into a blonde-haired cherub, and Drake stayed black-eyed with thick black hair. He didn't look like either of our parents. We didn't look like twins at all.

We seemed close over video, but it seemed to concern my parents. I crawled after Drake like a little-lost puppy, and I laughed as we played roughly. It seemed like harmless toddler play to me. Drake did like to take my toys, but it seemed like I liked to wrestle with him just as much as he liked to wrestle with me. I was always laughing, and it never seemed like I was being hurt on the videos.

It seemed to scare the shit out of my parents. They didn't think it was a twin bond. They seemed concerned that I would follow Drake wherever he went and they seemed to think our harmless wrestling would lead to him hurting me for real. They never actually said those words. They never voiced those fears. I just picked it up from repeated phrases on the videos.

"She's following him again."

"Drake plays too rough with her."

"It's like she's not trying hard enough to fight back when they are wrestling."

They never gave me any clues about why the Rothledges and the Lambs shouldn't mix. Lizzie and I watched video after video of Drake and I playing and my parents flipping out that I seemed to love my twin. Drake loved me too. On the video, it looked like we had a game. Drake would steal my toy, and I would have to wrestle him to get it back. Even when he always won, I'd get my toy back. We both seemed to enjoy this game, but my parent's commentary seemed more and more concerned.

They never said anything on video that would give me a hint. They never said anything that would tell me why me and Drake's playing concerned them so much. I grew more and more frustrated as I watched videos on the flash drives and got no answers. Before I knew it, the dates on the drives skipped six months. My parents recorded us often.

It was in that six-month window my twin disappeared, and I ended up in Kentucky. The rest of the flash drives were just still photos of me and written reports from a private investigator my parents hired to watch me. I only read a few, but they were very detailed. My parents were totally aware of the fact that the majority of the foster homes I ended up at, I was sleeping on a mattress on the floor in a room with six other kids.

I turned the computer off after only reading the investigators reports up until I was six. The investigator wrote about me like some science project. He wrote about *the child* never having seconds for dinner, never having a birthday party, having Santa ruined at an early age, getting picked on for wear too big boy's clothes, getting picked on for being an orphan, like he was just writing about the weather.

My parents didn't keep any more videos. They didn't keep notes. I had no gauge of what their reaction was to where they sent me because as much as they seemed to detail the first two years of my life, they just stopped after they sent me away. I could tell they loved me from the videos they did take.

The videos weren't just them documenting Drake and me together. There were a lot of videos of my mother singing me to sleep or braiding my hair. There were videos of my father playing games with me. It was quite obvious on the screen they loved me. There were videos of them doing the same things with Drake, but he didn't respond the way I did to my parent's attention. Drake only smiled with me.

Lizzie saw the same videos I did and already knew what I was thinking. With Lizzie, I never had to say a word. The secret room was getting too small. In reality, it was bigger than my bedroom in Kentucky, but it felt like the walls were closing in. Drake hissed and leapt off Lizzie's lap when she grabbed my hand.

"Okay, so we have a level ten clingy stalker, dumped by the man of your dreams, no tips all night and the rent is due all at once situation here. Except now, we don't have to make do with five-dollar pizza and cheap vodka. We're raiding your parent's bar, and now you've got an arsenal of servants to make us comfort food."

"Add a man I actually know here for a totally non-committal booty call that doesn't lead to anything, and I might forget about this for about two hours," I said, following her to the kitchen.

Chapter 7

When Jana saw how upset I was, she just shooed us away. Lizzie and I found the alcohol stash and were mixing drinks. My parents had a *lot* of good booze I'd only read about, but my bar didn't have. When I got my money, I was giving Jana and the rest of the staff a raise. While Lizzie and I were getting shit faced, they cooked us this huge, elaborate meal and a fucking cake. Like, this cake that looked like it could have been served at some celebrity wedding, and it was just for Lizzie and me because I had a shitty day.

I'm sure they all thought I was insane because as soon as I saw that two-layer fondant thing with pink icing roses all over it, I was already piss drunk. I burst into tears, starting hugging everyone, and professing my love for them. That was one of the few things Lizzie and I differed in. Lizzie was an angry drunk, and I loved everyone and everything once I was all liquored up. I told the staff, the cake, and the food I loved it, then I picked up a wailing Drake and danced around the kitchen telling him I loved him too.

I pigged out on cake and food, then apparently the butler and valet I didn't know I had carried Lizzie and me up to my parent's suite and put us to bed. I passed right the fuck out until really late the next day. When I finally woke up, Drake was sitting on my chest looking impatient. He glanced towards the sitting room like he wanted me to go to that secret room.

I was hungover as hell, and that room was going to have to wait. My head was pounding, and the small sliver of light from the curtains was hurting my eyes. Lizzie was still snoring next to me, and that damned cat had to start wailing again because he wanted me in that room.

I knew Drake hadn't pointed me in the wrong direction so far, but he was a cat and didn't understand human hangovers. I thought I was just going to have to deal with a wailing hairless cat, but then I heard shouting outside the bedroom door. Jana was screaming at someone, trying to keep them out. What fresh hell was this?

My new bedroom door flung open, and Mattan came bursting in. His eyes were wild, and I finally saw what Lizzie saw on the plane. Mattan was older than my parents would have been and I thought he was totally harmless when I invited him in. My creep radar was normally perfect, and I've got no idea how I missed that hungry glint in his eye. It wasn't sexual, at least not where I was concerned. Mattan wanted something from me. And I thought he knew exactly what happened to my twin and why I was sent away.

I was starting to doubt Drake was some sort of familiar or protector. He jumped off my chest and started rubbing against Mattan's legs purring up a storm. I was still in my clothes from yesterday, and my head was pounding, but apparently, Mattan needed a little boundary lesson.

"You'd better having a very fucking good reason for not only coming over here without calling first, but breaking into my bedroom while I'm trying to sleep."

Mattan looked utterly shocked. "So, the Lamb is really the Lion. Curious."

"Get the fuck out my bedroom!" I yelled, pointing at the door. "You will wait in the living room until I'm ready to see you, you're actually going to tell me what you know this time, and if Lizzie is with me when I get down there, you're going to look at her like she's your daughter and not creep her out again. Get it?"

"As you wish. I apologize," Mattan said, bowing his head. "I suppose I was so rude because I was curious what you had discovered."

What I'd discovered? I was pretty sure Mattan already knew the answer, I just didn't know why he was making me work for it. Or what that comment about the lamb and lion meant. It sounded like something one of my more religious foster families would spout.

Lizzie snored her way through Mattan's visit and me yelling. She wasn't the nicest person to wake up, and she was probably hungover as hell. Her moral support would be nice, but we didn't have to do everything together. And she needed her sleep just as much as I did.

I took a quick shower and dressed for battle. I wanted Mattan scared of me, and I didn't think he scared easily. He probably thought I was some helpless female and I'd dealt with his kind before. I pulled on my leather trousers with the metal grommets down the side. I had a purple belt that matched my hair with huge spikes on it. I buckled up my favorite steampunk bondage corset that always made me feel like a badass. The last thing was battle hair, and then I was ready to go down and confront Mattan.

I was ready to kick ass and take names. I was going to put Mattan in his place. I was going to *make* him tell me the secrets he was hiding. I was going to force it out of him why I ended up in Kentucky and where my twin was. I was—so confused. I expected Mattan to be waiting for me to yell at him and instead, he was sitting by a table spread with papers and my traitorous new cat sitting on his lap making sweet eyes and headbutting him.

Mattan grinned at me like a snake. I've got no idea how he had me so fooled before as the kindly, middle-aged family lawyer before to get me here. And why was the fucking cat so in love with him?

"I have all the paperwork to move everything in your name. I've handled everything with the bank. All it needs is your John Hancock, and everything is yours."

It was like a light switch went off, and Mattan was the kindly man I trusted enough to let him my living room when I was stark naked.

"No! Stop that. I want the man who burst into my bedroom back. There are some things I want to say to him. Just because you can turn it off doesn't mean there's shit I need to get off my chest."

Benedict Arnold, the cat, was purring so loud, he could have been shaking the walls, and Mattan still looked like a harmless old man scratching under his chin.

"Can I confess something I didn't tell you on the plane, Tabitha? There are thirteen families, and we've all mixed at some point. Your father's blood runs in my veins. My family married into the Lamb's several decades ago. Anyway, finding out there's a missing Lamb means there's a missing Adler too. I found the flash drives and the reports. Your twin, Drake, he's a part of my family too. I want to find him. Family is important to all of us."

My finely-honed bullshit radar didn't seem to work with Mattan. I had no family. I had no idea if a lost family member could make someone react the way he did barging into my bedroom. Then, I remembered Lizzie.

"That doesn't explain the eye fuck you gave my friend on the plane." It explained why he had no interest in my tits, but not why he made my friend uncomfortable. That was something I couldn't let pass.

"I apologize for how I treated your friend on the plane. It was unbecoming of a man my age to look at her like that. I was acting like Benjy, and he was on that plane as punishment. I apologize for bursting into your bedroom. The staff here will keep your family's secrets to their graves. I was hoping you had found something or they'd shared something with you so we could bring Drake home too. I worry about the boy. I know where you ended up. He could be someplace worse."

That made sense, but there was still something telling me not to trust Mattan. "I heard you had a falling out with my parents. What happened?"

"You know there's some big myth surrounding the Rothledges and the Lambs getting together? The entire Adler family was against the marriage and was quite vocal against it. My family wasn't the only one. There is an Adler who is an elder. She came up with a solution and told only your parents. It was the only way the elder council would sanction the marriage. I'm afraid it soured your parents against my entire family. Whatever was said to them, I don't know. I would have probably been against it, but I was caught up in family feuds."

"Would the elders have done something to Drake? How do you know the condition for them marrying was that they never have children and that was why me and Drake were kept a secret? The elders did something to Drake, and that was why I was sent away."

It seemed so obvious, and I had no idea why Mattan hadn't figured that out. Or why he brought me back here if I was going to be in danger from a bunch of toddler killing elders.

"No, I talked to them before I made any move to bring you here. Whatever my relative told your parents, the rest of the elders weren't aware, and she's dead now. They want answers just as much as the rest of us. When things settle down a little, they want to meet you just to talk."

How to ask about Drake, the cat without sounding totally insane. Was there some sort of secret code language to ask something along the lines of *hey, did a weird looking cat give you the computer password?* Didn't super-rich families like these throw you in an insane asylum so you wouldn't embarrass them if you thought the cat was talking to you?

"What can you tell me about the cat?" I asked.

"He's a peculiar, curious thing, isn't he? With the falling out with the families, the Adlers weren't invited to your family's parties, but I'd hear stories later about their cat. No matter how ill-behaved he was at parties, your parents never put him in his room. He hated everyone who wasn't a Rothledge or a Lamb and would attack if they tried to pet him or got too close. He must be able to sense my connection to the Lambs because he took to me right away. Why, is he attacking you?"

"No, Lizzie has this theory that I'm a witch and he's my familiar."

Mattan perked up way too much for my liking. "Why, are you able to communicate with him?"

"No, but it feels like he's trying. It's like he's been wanting me to go to this secret room in my parent's bedroom."

'Well, it's your bedroom now. Magical powers are not the silliest thing that has been suggested in our history. There have been tons of theories as to what was burned in the elder's secret room in the Salem Witch Trials. Most of the families have cats or special pets, but your parents had to have done a lot of research for this particular cat. Your parents would have gotten their hands on one of the first Peterbalds, and they had him shipped from Russia."

"How did you know there was a secret room in the study and get into the computer?" I demanded. Lizzie saw the same thing I did, but I needed to know there wasn't a slow carbon monoxide leak in the house or something and I just hallucinated the entire thing.

"Well, most of us have secret rooms in the study. It's sort of like an office for us. That was the first place I looked. As for the password, I hired someone to crack it for me. How did *you* get past the log in? I haven't given you the password yet."

"You wouldn't believe me if I told you."

"Seeing as how this conversation started by you asking me about the cat, if he got you into the computer and he wants you to look at the room in the bedroom, you should listen to him. Maybe he is a familiar, maybe he's something else, but he saw things in this house no one else saw and it sounds like he's trying to show you. I know how insane this all sounds, but right now, the cat is the only lead we have," Mattan said, shrugging.

Drake let out this little warble like he totally agreed with Mattan and I was starting to doubt the sanity of everyone in this house. Especially me because as soon as Mattan left, I was going to try to see if there was anything else Drake might want to show me.

"There's a ton of paperwork to sign to get everything signed over to you. We're going to need Lizzie down here because I thought ahead seeing how close the two of you were. Your parents have six cars, and I just thought you might want Lizzie to have one. I know you do everything together, but she might want to explore on her own and do might you."

"You'd really let me just *give* Lizzie a car? I don't have to ask permission from these elders and sign away part of my soul?"

Mattan chuckled. "This will be your house and the bank account is totally yours. If you wanted to keep all of the cars or sell them, that's up to you. If you don't want Lizzie to have a car, I can tear up the paperwork."

"Let me go wake her ass up. She should get to pick her new car. And both of us are going to have to learn to drive."

"It's normally a father's job to teach his daughter to drive, but I'd be happy to teach the both of you."

He was back to being the kindly middle-aged man again. He'd given me some good advice, and he made sure Lizzie got some of my good fortunes. He explained the falling out with my parents and given me the answers he had.

I went to get Lizzie to pick a car, so we could start signing papers. Mattan still confused me. He never set off my bullshit radar, and it seemed like he was telling me the truth about everything.

So, why was there something about him that just screamed I shouldn't trust him?

Chapter 8

We really should have been going to the secret room in my new bedroom. I already knew I didn't want Mattan in there with us. Mattan said *a few papers,* but he really wanted me to sign the equivalent of *War and Peace*. My hand hurt after signing so many documents. He had six documents for Lizzie's potential new car, and we spent an hour in the garage trying to pick.

Neither of us knew anything about cars because we never looked into them. What was the point in researching something you never thought you'd own? The cars in the garage looked expensive with custom paint jobs. I knew I wanted the sleek black one as soon as I laid eyes on it and hoped Lizzie didn't pick that one.

She walked around and had to sit in each one, but I already knew she was going to pick that custom pink classic car in the back. Mattan informed us it was a mustang and had a brand-new engine and air conditioning system. It belonged to my mother. I was happy for Lizzie and could picture her speeding through town in it with the top down once we learned to drive.

I knew I needed to be getting to that secret room in my new bedroom, but signing all that paperwork and picking cars took all day. Jana had another huge elaborate dinner fixed for us. I knew she wanted to fatten Lizzie and me up and bit, but we weren't thin just because we were dirt poor. We were both hot wired to run fast and had high metabolisms. When we did five-dollar pizza night, we both put a large away *each*.

By the time we were done eating, signing papers, and picking cars, I didn't want to explore that room just yet. Lizzie missed that entire conversation with Mattan, and I wanted to get her input. If I missed something, Lizzie always caught it. Jana sent us off to the master suite with a huge box of truffles. The chocolate here was so much better than a fun sized bag of M&Ms when I wanted chocolate.

I ran my entire conversation with Mattan by Lizzie as we shoved chocolate in our face holes.

"I don't get it, Lizzie. When I first met him, I trusted him enough to let him in and hear him out. The more I get to know him, everything in me is screaming he's up to something. I didn't get any vibes he was lying to me, but maybe there's something he's leaving out."

"Well, that explains why he didn't check out your rack. You've got amazing tits. I don't know, Tabby. Normally, when you're getting creeper vibes off someone, I get them too. I got them on the plane, but he apologized to me when we were alone looking at cars, and he seemed like he meant it. He hasn't stared at me like that again. It seems like he's trying to help. Maybe being in this house is activating your witchy powers— Drake, the sense you can't trust Mattan."

"Right, but Drake loves Mattan. You should have seen the two of them on the couch. If I'm somehow a witch and Drake is my familiar, shouldn't he be warning me about Mattan if something is off with him?"

Speak of the devil. I must not have closed the door all the way because Drake came strolling in like he knew we were talking about him. He seemed to like Lizzie even if everything I knew about him was that he hated anyone who wasn't family. He purred up a storm when she scratched his chin. It just sort of hit me. Drake accepted Lizzie because Lizzie was important to me.

I needed to start listening to Drake because clearly, he was no ordinary cat. Mattan said I should listen to Drake, and I didn't trust Mattan, but I'd always trusted my gut. My gut was telling me no matter how crazy I thought I was, there was something deeper to Drake than just a bald, bat-eared cat.

Drake had been pushing me and doing a lot of bitching in the that weird, hoarse voice of his to get me to the secret room in my parent's bedroom. Drake thought there was something in there I needed to see. Maybe all the answers about me and my twin were in that room.

    Tomorrow, I needed to focus all my efforts on that room. After breakfast, I was spending all day in that room and seeing what Drake had been trying to show me this entire time.

Chapter 9

I actually set the alarm and was up early. I wasn't working until three in the morning anymore, so there was no reason I couldn't start keeping normal, human hours anymore. I know most normal, human hours involved getting up much earlier, but I set my alarm for ten. Baby steps for now. I wasn't used to my parent's alarm. It started screeching at ten, and I bolted awake. I hadn't set an alarm since high school.

"Kill it with fire!" Lizzie shrieked, throwing her pillow at the alarm clock.

I was planning on hitting the snooze button a few times, but now the alarm was on the floor well away from the bed. I wondered about that damned cat again when he scurried into my bedroom. I *know* I shut the door before bed this time. Drake gave me this scathing look and pressed a button. The alarm clock stopped screaming.

Ten was late for most people, but it was early for me, even if I tried to go to bed early last night. I went to crash back into my pillow and landed in teeth and claws.

"Drake!" I yelled, flying out of bed.

He let out another one of those weird noises he liked to make and looked towards the sitting room. I put my hands on my hips and glared at him.

"Can I eat first, asshole?"

Jana must have heard the racket I was making. She stuck her head in the room.

"Are you hungry Tabitha? Just to warn you, I saw how angry you got with Mattan. Drake will need his monthly bath soon. Unless he trusts you to do it, Mattan will need to come over."

I grinned at that shit head cat. A little payback was in order. "How about breakfast, then I try to give him his bath?"

"He's going to need extra care with his baths. He requires daily wipe downs with cat wipes. Mattan has been doing it, but the past two days have been skipped. You have to rub him down with coconut oil before the shampoo and take extra care with his toes and tail. The water needs to be just the right temperature, and you have to get him out of the water and into the towel quickly, so he doesn't get sick. Since it's winter, once he's totally dry, he's going to need his sweater."

I groaned. I'd never had a spa treatment in my life, and this damned cat was getting coconut oil massages. I'm sure whatever shampoo was in there didn't come from the Dollar Store like mine did. And it was like he knew the word *bath* too because as soon as I said I was giving him one, he darted out the room and disappeared. And there were probably fifty million places to hide in this house not including all the secret rooms I didn't know about.

Jana saw me looking around for the damned cat. "Why don't you eat first? Drake thinks he's smart, but he always hides in the same place. Probably because it's such a huge pain to drag him out of there and there's a rug for him to dig his claws into. How about waffles for breakfast?"

My experience with waffles involved pulling them out of a box from the freezer and sticking them in the toaster. I was guessing the waffles here didn't come from a box that said *Eggo* on it and were probably covered in fresh fruit or chocolate or some shit. And I desperately wanted them. I loved those frozen waffles growing up, and I had to get up early to get one otherwise there would be an empty box. Lizzie would want to hear this because she loved those boxed waffles too.

I used to do this to Lizzie when we were sixteen, and I managed to get to the kitchen before the stampede. I leaned next to her ear.

"Waffles, Lizzie," I said sweetly.

She bolted to a sitting position like we were sixteen and going to have to fight someone for a frozen waffle again. Her hair was sticking up everywhere, and she looked ready to punch someone.

"Jana's making waffles," I said, grinning.

Jana was looking at us like we both had seven heads each. "If I'd known you girls liked them, I would have made them yesterday. How do you like them?"

Lizzie groaned and rubbed her neck. "Without someone stealing mine out the toaster."

Jana finally realized what was going on. "How about with chocolate hazelnut, strawberries, and whipped cream? We make Belgian waffles here."

"Oh, my god, that so makes up for giving Drake a bath," I moaned, licking my lips.

Jana disappeared, and Lizzie and I started getting dressed. "You're really going to try to give him a bath?"

"Everyone says he only likes family members. I know Mattan is a distant relative, but there's just something about him that makes me want to stick my boot up his ass and kick him out the house. I'd rather try to do it myself before calling him."

Lizzie shrugged. She threw on an old pair of leggings and a t-shirt and pulled her hair into a ponytail. "I seem to be an exception to Drake's family rule. Maybe if you can't do it, he'll let me."

"You really want to try after we found out he's traumatized most of the groomers here that are used to bad animals?"

"Drake's not so bad. He seems to be intelligent and trying to show us things. Maybe he sensed something about the groomers. They say animals can sense things about people."

"Every groomer in Salem, though? Seems unlikely."

"Cats are weird. Before we met, I was in this foster family that had this cat. She would just sit there and destroy a toilet paper roll if you left the bathroom door open."

"Well, Jana said she knows Drake's hiding place, and it's a bitch to get him out. I guess I'll have to get over my thing and finally see his room. His hiding place is probably in there."

"Girl, you've got a lot of *things* you need to deal with. You haven't even looked at your own fucking old room or your twin's room. I'm betting that the door on the right leads to your room and the door to the foot of the bed leads to your twins. Or the other way around."

"Lizzie, do you want to bring up twenty-six years of fucked up or do you want to go eat waffles that didn't come from the freezer and let me do this on my own time?"

"Let's go eat waffles, bitch. And you're going to owe me big if I end up bathing Drake. He's not neutered, and those little balls are gross."

"Ew! Isn't it just like, responsible pet ownership to cut their balls off?"

"Maybe Drake does those cat beauty pageants? Have you ever watched them on TV? It's like Miss America for cats and dogs. I don't think they do that for those things."

"Do I want to know how you know that?"

"The cat that went all psychopath on the toilet paper? My foster parents at that home liked to watch those. It was kind of nice. Instead of the Superbowl, we watched the Puppy Bowl. I hate sports."

We started making our way down to the kitchen. "That's kind of a lie, you know," I pointed out. "When the bar tried to get more customers by doing oiled up bikini wrestling, your tongue was practically hanging out your mouth."

"Hey, I dated the champion for six months. That's like ten years in my time."

"Oh, my Lord," I said when we got downstairs. I had totally forgotten about bikini wrestling and Lizzie's habit of blowing through girlfriends.

There was a plate in the center of the table piled high with these beautiful waffles. They'd made enough for us to totally pig out and not have to punch someone for the last one. I loved Lizzie to death, but we'd scrapped over the last waffle before. There was a jar of chocolate hazelnut butter, white chocolate hazelnut butter, fresh strawberries and bananas, and what looked like a bowl of fresh whipped cream.

Lizzie and I totally forgot about bathing Drake or me dealing with my shit and looking at both the secret room and my old bedroom. We were squealing and giggling, talking about all the times we were victorious and got to the damned waffles before they were all gone. They weren't anything like this. We stuck them in the toaster and shoved them in our faces with nothing on them, so someone didn't come running in and yank it out our hands.

In certain houses, it didn't matter if you put it in the toaster or hell, if it was even if your hand. Certain foods were coveted and going to get stolen. Waffles, Hot Pockets, Pizza Bagel Bites. Any kind of junk food that went in the microwave that wasn't a bologna or ham sandwich, of which there were plenty.

That was when it finally hit me. Lizzie and I still ate sandwiches because they were cheap, filling, and the supplies would last a while. I actually hated bologna sandwiches. Peanut butter wasn't much better. I never had to eat one again if I didn't want to. I never had to eat anything from a box in the microwave again.

I got up and hugged Jana. I was trying not to cry. She probably had no idea what she was doing when she suggested waffles.

"Whatever all of you are being paid, I'm doubling it. You've all been so nice, and I never thought anything like this would happen to me."

Jana just laughed and hugged me back. "Remind me to cook you waffles again when you need cheering up."

Chapter 10

I was a little shocked when Jana showed me Drake's room. It adjoined to my new room, what would have been Drake, my twin's room. It was furnished for a prince. There was a king sized four poster bed on a dais, just like in my new room. It was weird. My new room was furnished with classical art. There were a lot of nude paintings and sculptures. Drake's room had crucifixes and a lot of religious paintings and sculptures on almost every surface.

It wasn't like that for the rest of the house. The art in the rest of the house looked expensive, but it seemed like it was pagan gods and goddesses or characters from stories. Drake's room was ornately furnished, and the art looked expensive, but it all looked like it was dealing with repenting and God's punishment of the wicked. It creeped me out a little considering this was supposed to be my twin's room.

I shot Jana a confused look. "Does my bedroom look like some sort of nunnery you send wicked children to?"

"They never got the chance to set up your bedroom. This was Drake's nursery, but you always coslept with your parents until the day you and Drake disappeared. Drake's room didn't look like this when he was a baby. It looked like a room appropriate for a baby."

Lizzie was peering at all the bloody torture scenes on the wall. "Is this just where they moved all the art that can ruin your dinner or did they buy it specifically for the cat?"

"All this art was scattered randomly around the house. Some of Tabitha's ancestors married gentiles. From what I've been told, this art was bought by gentiles that married into the family. Your parents moved it all into this bedroom after the children disappeared. Your parents didn't really come in here after you and Drake disappeared. They stood at the door and called to the cat, and he would come out. Drake is going to be right under that huge bed, in the middle. He never fought your parents for baths, but Drake's vets did home visits. He was always under the bed."

"Who got him out if my parents didn't come in here?"

"Well, the vet had this kind of pole thing with a claw that got him out in a way that didn't hurt him, but it pissed Drake right off. They had to put him in sort of this net thing, then sedate him for his vet visits."

"Is that why he still has his little cat balls?" Lizzie asked.

"Probably. There are no female cats here, and Drake was always good about using the litter box and never spraying, so I guess they just never did it."

"Well, we don't have a claw, and I don't think any of us wants to risk facial scarring to get under there and get him," I said.

"I know just the thing," Jana said, going to a huge armoire.

She pulled out a bag of treats and started shaking it. When she unzipped the bag, my nose was assaulted by the stench of tuna, and I was about to tell her to close it, but Drake came flying out from under the bed. I pounced on him and cradled him in my arms. Jana popped a treat in his mouth and told me she'd already run his bath.

Drake started fighting as soon as he saw the sink. When I went to pull his little green sweater off, he launched himself at my head. I shrieked and flailed. Drake was caught in my hair.

"Shit, Lizzie! The cat is possessed!"

Drake was scratching up my neck and ears, and both of us were howling. Lizzie managed to get him off me. Drake practically threw himself over her shoulder in a kitty hug, panting. Lizzie wrapped her arms around him and stroked his head.

"Oh, *sure!*" I snapped. "I traumatized *you.*"

Lizzie easily pulled his sweater off. Judas Cat clearly only wanted baths from Lizzie. I just rolled my eyes. Lizzie shot me a helpless look.

"I'll bathe him. Maybe he's still mad because you haven't looked at that room yet. Go look at that room, and I'll give him his bath," Lizzie said.

"Traitorous bastard cat," I muttered, stomping off to my new bedroom.

What was with that? I was family. He was trying to show me things, but he didn't want me bathing him? Were all cats so strange?

I knew where the secret panel was this time. This time, when the secret door opened, I walked inside.

CHAPTER 11

This secret room was huge — almost the size of my new bedroom. I looked around. This one also looked like a study, but it looked like it was full of relics. There were paintings of lions and weird sheep with eyeballs all over the place. This time, everything was on paper. It looked like there were weird graphs and ideas sketched all over the desk, but it was probably in Hebrew, and I had no idea what it said.

I seemed to look through paper for ages before Drake strolled in and hopped on the desk. He was strolling all over my papers like he didn't think I needed to be looking at those. When he sufficiently had my attention, he gave me a hoarse meow.

"What, asshole? You want to attack me again?"

I swear, that cat turned this nose up at me. He hopped on a chest on the corner of the desk. I hadn't noticed it because it was covered in papers. It wasn't locked. I guess my parents didn't think it needed to be because it was in a secret room.

There was four thin, stone circles and they looked hand carved. I set them on the desk and studied them. One had a bow and a crown. The other had a sword. I studied the last two. One had a pair of scales on them, and the last was utterly blank. The carvings were highly detailed, and the stone was almost wafer thin. It seemed impossible to me to put that amount of detail into the carving without totally breaking the stone.

I was about to pick one up to study it in greater detail. Drake was sitting in front of all the stones. Right before I could reach for the one with the bow and crown, that asshole looked me right in the eye and swatted it off the desk. I fumbled, but it slipped through my fingers and fell to the hardwood floor. I bolted back up, determined to save at least one of those stones. They were probably priceless family heirlooms. Every single stone slid through my hands and crashed to the hard floor.

"Damn it, Drake, I'm getting you neutered if you don't behave!" I yelled, bending over to survey the damage.

The stone circles were either in pieces or cracked in half. I could see a huge flash of light above my head on the desk, and I wouldn't put it past Drake to have set the entire fucking room on fire. Maybe he led me here to destroy evidence. I bolted back upright, and there were four strange men sitting on the couch in the sitting room. Four *hot* men, but I also didn't know them and had no idea who let them in.

They were all eyeing me curiously. One of them had skin like the blackest night and dark eyes. Another was deathly pale and was totally bald. There was a ginger in the group with green eyes, and the other man looked like he just walked off the set of *Lord of the Rings* playing a Light Elf. They all had to be over six foot five and were ripped with muscle. Focus, Tabitha. Every foster home you've been in cared enough to tell you not to take candy from strange men.

"Who the fuck are you?" I demanded.

All four men cracked up laughing. The *Lord of the Rings* reject was staring at me like he was undressing me as I stood behind that huge desk and tried to stare them down.

"Well, aren't you just the sexist little Lamb we've come across so far?" he purred.

"Watch it," the bald man said. "I think we've got the Lion this time."

Mattan had said something exactly like that to me, and there were fucking lions and lambs all over this damned room. I was starting to think Mattan found me because he wanted to know what was in this room and these men were related to him. I knew I couldn't trust that man.

"How exactly are you related to Mattan?" I demanded. "If you give me an actual real answer, I'll just kick you out instead of breaking the heel of my boot off in your ass on the way out the door."

The ebony skinned man just winked at me. "Mattan will be punished for his part in all of this, though I will tell you, there's been a debate for twenty-six years whether to punish him or reward him for orchestrating everything. In the end, I suppose it's up to you."

I tried to let my anger slip away. Whoever these men were, they had answers about me and my twin. "Do you know where my brother is?"

"Of course. He's right here. I believe he just tricked you into opening the four seals and starting the apocalypse. You're looking at The Four Horsemen. Well, the modern-day equivalent. We have the appropriate sports cars in your garage instead of horses," the elf reject said.

"Is this some fucking joke? Do you *want* to see what happens when I need to maim a man?"

He threw back his head and laughed. "Oh, sweetie, you want to toe to toe with Conquest? I'd love having you underneath me to prove a point."

"Please," I scoffed. "You're probably a two-pump chump who goes all stalkerish after a pity fuck and needs a restraining order."

The man with the shaved head was now laughing. "Best not poke this one. She's probably not into ass play the same way you are."

The ginger finally spoke. "You're *all* poking her. This is all new for her. We should just tell her the truth. It's already going to be hard for her to believe. She didn't grow up here, remember?"

"I refused to call you The Four Horsemen. Do you actually have real names?"

The light elf stood. "I'm the Horseman of Conquest. God, that sounds so much better than the people that call me Pestilence. Like I bring cockroaches to the apocalypse. My symbol is a bow and a crown, not a can of Raid. I vanquish and now people associate me with pests. It's fucking insulting."

"Well, you've got baggage, do you have an actual name? I refuse to call you Conquest because I don't want you getting any ideas."

"I go by Chase," he said, grinning. "Honey, once you get to know me, you'll be begging me to be my conquest."

"Baggage and an ego? No thanks," I snapped. He was sexy as hell, and if I could have had a group thing with all the actors in their makeup playing the elves in that movie, I totally would have done it, but I had enough baggage of my own.

The ginger who actually tried to help me stood up. His hair was flaming red, and he wore it shorter than Chase, but it was still in his eyes. I always had a thing for the gingers, and I wanted to brush his bangs out his eyes. I had to remind myself all these men were insane and thought they were the Four Horsemen of the Apocalypse and were seriously going to play this out with me.

"I already know you don't believe us and will require proof. I promise you to give you all the answers. You may call me Gideon."

Gideon just sat back down. I knew I was going to regret asking this. "And which Horseman are you claiming to be?"

I finally saw a smile from him. And some of the cheek from the rest of them. "War. Do you want to see my sword?"

The bald man stood up. He totally pulled off the bald look. He looked like a bouncer from one of the better bars I couldn't afford to drink at. He was dressed like it too. Leather pants and a leather vest. When I looked around, I realized all four of them wore a lot of black leather: even Chase, the elf man.

"Guess which Horseman I am, and I'll tell you my name," he boomed, his bright blue eyes sparkling. Baldy's voice was sexy as hell, but I wasn't playing this game.

"You're assuming I actually know anything about Horsemen and apocalypses. It's was the fucking apocalypse back home for Lizzie and me back home when our roots were showing, and we couldn't afford hair dye. It was the apocalypse when we were on the last package of microwaved noodles, and we got shit tips and couldn't afford food. My entire childhood was the apocalypse, so I didn't bother reading up on end of the world theories. I wish all of you would just get to the point. I don't like this game."

"I'm Death, and you can call me Bash. As Gideon said, we'll explain everything to you. I'm sorry, Tabitha. It's just so nice being on Earth again, we're cutting up a little, and you're taking the brunt of it. Where is your friend Lizzie now?"

"Probably bandaging her hand if Drake mauled her or taking a shower after giving him a bath."

The last man stood. "My name is Zed and I guess you would say I have baggage like Chase. I'm the Horseman of Justice, but everyone likes to call me Famine now. I balance the scales; I don't destroy food. I'm rather fond of Earth food. Things have changed since the last time I was here, and I'm interested in trying some new dishes."

Every single man stopped talking, and I followed their gaze to the door. Lizzie was standing there with her arms crossed and an eyebrow cocked.

"I know I took a long soak in the bathtub, but did you find a hot dude delivery service here in Salem?"

"How *did* you get in here? No one would have let you in my bedroom. I haven't been here long, but they would have made you wait downstairs and come and got me."

Gideon was staring pretty hard at Drake. "Did you get a good look at the seals before they broke? Remember what we told you and the symbols you saw. We were yanked here as soon as the seals broke."

I wasn't playing this game anymore. "You said you knew where my twin was. Where is he?"

All eyes were on the cat now.

"Sitting right there on the desk in that green sweater. Drake, you know you weren't supposed to trick her. Care to make yourself known now?"

I must have been going crazy. I heard a voice in my head.

"Hello, twin."

Chapter 12

I just stared down at the cat and didn't move. I wasn't sure if I'd made up that voice in my head or I'd inherited some cosmic shitstorm with this house.

"My human body is in a coma in another secret room. Now that the Horsemen are out, you can put me back in. Do you think Lizzie would date me once I'm human again?"

"You little shit! You mauled me because you're into Lizzie?"

"Wait, what?" Lizzie said. "If anyone here is into me, it needs to be said that none of you have boobs and I'm not interested."

"*Drake the cat* is talking to me in my head. These four assholes are telling me he's really my twin. *He's* telling me I can put him human again. *I'm* telling everyone in this room I'm going to need a really strong drink."

"Put me back in my body, Tabby. I've never been drunk before."

"You stop talking to me in my head, Drake! If you tricked me into starting the apocalypse, you're probably stuck in that fucking cat for a very good reason!"

I was bordering on hysterical, and I *never* got hysterical. Gideon got up and wrapped his arm around my shoulder. He shot the cat a look.

"Really, Drake. Enough! You could have waited until Tabitha was here more than a few days and managed to find out a little more about her past before you sprung the damned apocalypse on her. Let's get you that drink, shall we?"

I leaned into Gideon's hard chest, and we all went down to the living room. Bash and Lizzie were arguing over who could make the better drink. I knew Bash thought he was being funny, but Lizzie would have thought he was being a sexist pig and thought a woman couldn't have possibly known how to mix a proper cocktail. I didn't want to hear it because when Lizzie got angry, she turned into a banshee and she'd probably break her hand punching Bash in the face.

"Bash, you make drinks for your friends and Lizzie can make mine. She knows what I like, and she works at a bar with me."

Pretty soon, we were all sitting on the huge sectional with drinks. I shooed Drake off Lizzie's lap when he went to curl up there. My twin was apparently a creeper. Zed leaned forward with his elbows on his knees.

"I'm sure you have a million questions, Tabitha. Where should we start?"

"All I was told was that none of the families knew about Drake and me and there's some urban legend about my parents missing. Does that urban legend have something to do with the cat having telepathy?"

"You were given background about the tribe and families? The families are all descendants. Your father's family, the Lambs, they descended from Judah. The original tribe mostly stayed the same, but they took in other families. Your mother's family, the Rothledges, they are descendants of Judas. The reason the two families were told never to mix was that at least one of their offspring would be the Antichrist."

"If Drake and I are twins, what does that mean? And why didn't my parents bother with fucking condoms if they knew one of their kids was going to be the damned Antichrist?"

"Your parents watched you as you grew. Drake was the Antichrist, and you were the Lamb of God. Drake can't open the seals. Only you can do that. Your parents knew. They saw you loved him and you followed him everywhere. They worried about what would happen when you were older. Drake would know who he was, but you wouldn't. They worried Drake would convince you to break all of the seals because you loved him. Your parents were scared one night. You and Drake were playing. He put a pillow over your face and sat on it. If they hadn't come in, you would have suffocated. You were both only two. They used old magic to put Drake in the cat and sent you away. I don't think they realized you'd grow up so strong-willed," Zed said, smiling.

"That still doesn't explain why Drake and I were born in the first place. I'm not even supposed to be giving birth to the damned Antichrist, and I double up on birth control, so I don't get pregnant."

"They actually did. The elder that gave your parents her blessing to marry did it with the condition your father get a vasectomy. This apocalypse, it's not right. It was forced. It was always supposed to happen in its own time. Elliot Lamb is not your father. Someone else with Lamb blood was aware of what would happen and raped your mother."

I already knew. He didn't have to tell me. It was the entire reason I was here. "Mattan," I growled. "It's the reason he's been trying to get me to trust him and the reason Drake likes him so much."

"Yes," Bash said, nodding. "The world is not ready for the apocalypse. It's not time yet. We come when the seals are broken, but what happens next it up to you, Tabitha."

"Why me and not Drake? Don't you answer to him?"

Chase grinned. "Actually, no. You and Drake are two sides to a coin. The Horsemen are not from hell like you seem to think. Drake has no control over us. It's up to *you* whether you break the other seals and start the apocalypse. Drake is here to trick you and make you doubt your judgment, so you *do* break the seals. The entire goal of the apocalypse is to create a new heaven and earth. Drake is here to prevent Satan from being bound and for the two of them to rule the new heaven and earth. We carry out your orders, not his. If you don't want us to do a thing except sit here and look pretty, we'll do that."

"So, what do we do with Drake? He apparently wants back in his body to creep on my best friend who isn't even interested in men."

Gideon cleared his throat. "Lizzie isn't just your best friend. None of us have any idea how this happened, but you and Lizzie are so close and have stuck together because Lizzie is part of the apocalypse too."

"What? I'm just an orphan from Kentucky."

"Clearly, not. You're one of the Witnesses. There's another one out there, and I'm guessing they ended up in foster care somewhere too. You probably have ties to Salem and the original families."

"You're not seriously going to tell me there are more than two secret babies here?"

"Not at all," Zed said. "Family members have left Salem, been disowned, and ended up all over the place. You could have been the child of a sixteen-year-old runaway or someone who left and couldn't take care of a child."

"How do we find out who Lizzie's parents are?" I asked.

Chase grinned at me. "We train and prepare while we wait. Conquest and War, in the modern age, aren't done much on the battlefield anymore. It's done from behind a computer. Between Gideon and me, we can hack anything because this wasn't supposed to happen right now. We can find out where Lizzie comes from. She deserves to know."

Lizzie and I exchanged glances and didn't have to say a word. *Nothing* came for free, and no one helped you unless there was something in it for them. Even this house didn't come for free. It came with the fucking Antichrist, and I had no idea if I was supposed to house and feed four Horsemen who looked like they could put away epic amounts of food or if I would be breaking some sort of heaven or hell protocol if I told them to get a hotel room. Did the Four Horsemen of the Apocalypse have debit cards?

All four men seemed to be able to read Lizzie and me just as well as we could read each other. They were all looking at me like they knew I thought they were full shit and I was figuring out how to give them the boot. I wanted to punch all four of them in the face because they were looking at us like they felt sorry for us.

"You and Lizzie need each other, and you both need all four of us to protect you from Drake," Zed said. "Mattan too. No one is happy Mattan jumped the gun on the apocalypse, but Mattan is going to try to help Drake. Drake will try to trick Tabitha, and it is written the Beast kills the Witness."

"So, why don't we just have the cat put to sleep?" I asked. Twin or not, I didn't know him, he'd been lying to me this entire time, and no one killed Lizzie except me.

"Because Drake can't be killed by a vet or anyone in this room. It's safest to keep him in the cat for now."

"Where *is* Drake?" Lizzie asked. "He's always been pretty reactive when we say anything about him. He would have mauled someone by now for plotting to kill him."

Lizzie was right. While we were talking and I was worried about that damned cat killing my soul sister, we'd all lost track of Drake.

Gideon stood up. It was like this wind developed that blew his hair back and don't ask me where the fuck that huge sword came from. Chase was sporting a huge bow. Zed and Bash both had nasty looking guns on them. They all had some sort of wind blowing their hair back, and I guess I couldn't deny they were actually who they said they were now. They looked the part, and there was only one place Gideon could have been hiding that sword, and he wouldn't have been able to sit.

"Spread out. Check the room Drake's body was in. Now that Drake knows Mattan is his father, he could have called to him. If Drake knows any of the secret ways in and out of this house, then Mattan does. Bash, stay with Tabitha and Lizzie while we check things out."

Bash went to stand in the archway and Lizzie, and I just stared at each other.

"Girl, just when I think our lives can't get more fucked up, your twin is the Antichrist stuck in a cat and now he might be on the loose."

CHAPTER 14

Well, we were certainly fucked. Sure, I had the Four Horsemen of the Apocalypse here with me, but Drake, both in his cat form and human form had shit the bed and disappeared. I was certain he was with his, well, *our* father and Mattan was trying to put him back together again like if Humpty Dumpty was actually the Antichrist. The problem was, no one knew if Mattan had that ability.

Everyone seemed to think I was safe. Mattan and Drake needed me to break the other seals to start the apocalypse. Lizzie voiced my opinion without me having to. I totally wasn't safe, and neither was Lizzie. They could capture both of us and force me so they wouldn't hurt her. The beast was supposed to kill Lizzie, and I wouldn't put it past Drake to turn her into some sort of sex slave first. Drake was technically a virgin and Lizzie was hot as shit. Everyone loved Lizzie, even if she mostly hated everyone and everything except blondes with big boobs who treated her like shit.

It had been two days since Drake disappeared. The Four Horsemen were both growing on me and annoying me. They all had totally distinct personalities. Chase had his baggage about how people saw his role, but he was Conquest all the way. He was a huge flirt, but he managed to do it in a way that didn't set off my creep radar at all like he did the first day. It was more this playful banter, and I'll be honest, it was working. The fact that he wore his white hair long and looked like an elf from a movie wasn't helping me keep any type of resolve not to fuck him.

Gideon was on guard the most with his sword, but he also insisted on helping Lizzie learn what she was supposed to be doing as a witness. I wasn't totally shocked when he told us both she was supposed to have the gift of prophecy, but we both thought it was totally badass when we found out she could breathe fire. Lizzie always seemed to know when to dump someone before they could dump her and she seemed to know with my relationships too. She also could have made bank predicting the weather.

Gideon was patient with both of us as we cut up and weren't acting as seriously as we should be while he tried to help us. Gideon was actually pulling double duty. He took turns not sleeping at night guarding the house, and when he wasn't helping Lizzie train, he was helping Chase find out where she came from. He was doing all of this for Lizzie, but I felt his eyes on me when he thought I wasn't looking.

Zed was Justice through and through. When it was his turn to guard Lizzie and me, we got an earful, and we knew he was an ally. Zed thought what happened to both of us growing up was horrible. Zed's rants were like my inner thoughts I hadn't said out loud yet. None of this would be happening right now if my parents had gotten me out of just one of the shitty situations I ended up in and prepared me for this. Drake would never have been able to trick me into breaking those seals if I had been warned about Drake. The child that followed Drake around like a puppy died after a few years growing up in the foster homes I ended up at. There were plenty of good foster homes, I just didn't get sent to any of them, and neither did Lizzie.

Zed was angry about our situation, but he kept saying my parents just didn't know better with what they had thrust on them. He blamed everything on Mattan. Zed was planning some epic justice for Mattan. He had several ideas, but he hadn't settled on one yet. He just kept saying Mattan fucked up the scales and he couldn't let that pass. He also wanted my permission for when Mattan got his due. They all wanted permission for everything. Having four hot men asking my permission for everything was going to give me a fat head.

Bash was not how I pictured Death at all. He looked like he could kill someone just by giving them stink eye, but he cut up more than Lizzie and me. Bash was fucking hilarious. Lizzie and I decided he was part of our tribe after a few hours of him guarding us, even if he wasn't a girl and didn't even remotely act like one. Bash may have even had a sicker sense of humor than I did and his favorite subject right now was hairless cat jokes and making fun of Drake being stuck in a cat for so long.

I thought we should be on the offensive, not the defensive. Lizzie and I both thought we should just storm Mattan's house, kill Mattan, and stick Drake in a frog this time. We were all gathered together, and I was voicing that opinion again.

"Tabby, love, if we storm Mattan's estate, he's probably got security cameras. We'd be playing right into Mattan and Drake's hands. Mattan and Drake could get control over you and Lizzie," Chase said, massaging my shoulders.

"Not if Mattan is dead and Drake is in a frog," I groaned, trying not to enjoy Chase's massage.

Lizzie was technically the only person allowed to call me Tabby, but all the guys had started, and I found it didn't piss me off.

I heard a deep, sexy chuckle behind me that could only belong to Bash. His voice did things to me. "If I'd known a backrub was the solution to get her to argue less, I would have tried that the first day she broke the seals."

Zed just rolled his eyes. "If you laid a hand on her, she would have made good on that threat to put her boot up your ass."

"The three of you have gotten a little too fond of flirting with Tabby instead of worrying about Mattan and Drake," Gideon said. I wished he would let loose everyone in a while. "Tabby is right though. Just because they haven't come here yet doesn't mean they aren't plotting. Mattan is a lawyer, and Drake is the Antichrist. Between the two of them, they could be coming up with anything."

"Do any of you know enough about the law to read the papers Mattan had Tabby sign?" Lizzy asked. "What if there's something in there that Tabby *has* to share this house with Drake? *That's* what the two of them could be up to. Trying to get Drake back in his body and planting him in the house. None of you have explained how Drake got into the cat in the first place. Figuring *that* out would tell us if they managed to make Drake a real boy again."

I finally saw a grin from Gideon. His facial features were sharp and angular. It was nice to see a grin on his face, especially a goofy one like that.

"Finally, the witness contributes something useful. Give it a few more days, and you'll be spewing prophecy and fire."

I knew Lizzie liked the Four Horsemen. Well, Lizzie liked *me* with the Four Horsemen. She thought with everything going on, I needed to get laid, and any one of them would do.

Lizzie just smiled sweetly at Gideon. "I wear taller heels than Tabby does."

I had no idea this was possible for him, but Gideon fell out laughing. "So, we need to explain Drake, the cat first," he said when he calmed down. "People didn't just make up witches and start burning people for no reason. They never actually burned a *real* witch as far as I know, but the families here in Salem kept several witches safe during the witch trials. Have you heard of familiars?"

Lizzie and I both grew up poor, but we had active library cards and read all the time. Nothing that would have prepared me for the apocalypse and Drake, but we both loved a good witchy paranormal story. We both nodding emphatically. We both knew various fictional theories, but I had a feeling Gideon was about to ruin our favorite genre and tell us the truth.

"The way familiars are normally made is by calling forth the spirit of an ancestor and asking the animal permission to allow the spirit in. Your mother broke several laws of nature putting Drake in the cat, but she kept Drake and Mattan apart. She should have picked another animal. It was Drake that tripped them when they fell down the stairs," Gideon explained.

My mouth was hanging open, but Lizzie was furious. "Just when I was starting to like you. You can't drop that bomb while you're trying to explain how Drake got into the fucking cat. Save the parricide until *after* we've got a full picture of how Tabby's twin got into a fucking cat in the first place. Got it, asshole?"

Gideon just sat there, looking shocked. He looked like he didn't know what to say. Bash walked over and walloped him over the head.

"Gideon, I'm Death, and even I have more sensitivity in my pinky than you do in your entire body. I'm putting you in time out. Let the rest of us talk for the rest of the day. How are you, Tabby? Do you need something? Waffles? A group hug? Do you want to punch Gideon?"

I don't know why I wasn't reacting that Drake killed my mother. I was pissed Gideon chose to drop it in the middle of the explanation of how Drake ended up in the cat, but I wasn't exactly shocked he committed murder. He was the Antichrist, and I was looking at the Four Horsemen of the Apocalypse because he tricked me.

"I'm not a baby, and I can mourn my mother *after* Drake and Mattan are taken care of. We still don't know how Drake got into the cat without anyone knowing about it. Drake said his body was in a coma in another room. That's not a spirit. Drake was a toddler when he was put in the cat. What exactly was taken out of the toddler and put into the cat and how?" I demanded.

Chase went back to massaging my shoulders. I guess they thought I was going to lose my shit because Zed grabbed my feet and hauled them into his lap. I wasn't wearing my fuck me boots today and was barefoot. Zed was just as good a foot massages as Chase was at backrubs. Gideon decided not to speak after Bash smacked him up the back of the head. Bash finished the story.

"What your mother did to Drake, it was in a book she burned as well as how to reverse it. What they did to Drake was not the first time it's been done. Sometimes, a witch will go dark. If they are spurned by a lover or someone shorts them in a deal enough to piss them off, they'd stick them in a toad and bury their body. Ever been told the wicked witch will turn you into a toad? There's some truth to that."

"So, why didn't my parent's bury Drake's body? Why did they keep in in a coma?"

"I suspect because they didn't know what would happen to it. Drake is only supposed to be able to die by being thrown into the lake of fire. But with him being put into a cat like that, I suppose they thought they neutralized him."

"So, that solves that with some unnecessary drama from Gideon. Do all of the families know the same spell my mother did? Does Mattan know?"

"I think it's safe to say if Mattan doesn't, Drake will. Drake made his move now because he had all the pieces," Zed said. "The Antichrist is cunning. Drake has always known who he was, even as a baby. You didn't. He was trying to gain your trust and love when you didn't know better. Your parents knew this. They didn't know you yet. I think you would have grown into a badass even if you stayed here and you could have been warned about Drake."

"If you don't want us storming Mattan's place because of security cameras and you claim you're such badasses with computers, why don't you just hack his system, so we know what's going on in there?" Lizzie asked.

All four of the Horsemen were grinning. Chase nearly threw me off the couch jumping to get to his computer. "If one witness is already helping, thinking about what we could do with the other one? Gideon, you work on trying to get into Mattan's security system. I'm focusing all my efforts into looking into Lizzie's past and trying to find the other witness."

Chapter 15

Esther and Odelia were kind to us my first day here, but I was shocked they hadn't come back here before now. Especially not with all the talk they gave us about introducing us to their daughters. They were in a huff when they came in, but they stopped and were eyeballing the four hunky Horsemen in the living room.

"Tabitha, really, whatever happened between you and your twin, you need to fix it. He's really such a lovely boy. He and Ariel have been talking, and I believe they are sweet on each other," Odelia fussed. "Does he not approve of your male friends? He seems so old-fashioned, like a knight out of the old stories."

So, Drake was whole, and he was already looking to get laid. And by all accounts, he'd moved on to someone who dressed like Lizzie. That was a little creepy, but I knew with Drake, it meant something. Drake went after Lizzie because she was a witness. Ariel was important somehow. Either that, or even the Antichrist was in a hurry to lose his V-card and had a thing for the Goth Lolita look.

I needed to turn on the same charm I used when I had a bunch of crabby ass, demanding customer I knew weren't going to tip me. Even with the whole *my brother is the Antichrist and tricked me into starting the apocalypse* thing, I was glad I didn't have to act like a performing monkey for a ten percent tip anymore.

"Odelia!" I said, taking her arm. "You promised to bring Ariel over days ago. Lizzie and I have been dying to meet Ariel and Natalia. Why did you bring them to Mattan's instead of here?"

Esther gave me this stern look. "Mattan called us. He said he located your twin finally and you don't want to share the house with him. Mattan is letting him stay, so the poor boy is not totally homeless. Really, Tabitha, this house is huge and you inherited so much. Surely, you can give a little to your twin."

"Esther, you've heard Mattan's side, but not mine. There are things about my brother he's not telling you. Trust me when I tell you Drake ran before we could talk things out. Did Mattan tell you the real truth about Drake and me?"

Lizzie pinched my arm, giving me a warning not to say too much. I'd started planning this speech as soon as I heard Drake was whole and had his sights on Ariel. I needed to get Ariel in front of my Horsemen and find out if she was the other witness. It had to be some huge longshot that both witnesses were into Lolita, but this situation was already pretty fucked up, and nothing would surprise me.

"Come sit, there are things I think Mattan left out," I said, leading her to the couch. Esther and Odelia were eye fucking the Four Horsemen, and I half wondered if anything I said was going to sink in. "Did Mattan tell you why my parents kept Drake and me a huge secret and then we both disappeared?"

Odelia finally stopped checking out Bash's biceps in his leather vests. "I was under the impression no one knew, not even you."

"The condition the elder gave my parents for getting married was that Elliot have a vasectomy. Elliot is not me and Drake's father. The reason Mattan had a falling out with Elliot and Levana was that he raped my mother. Drake is with Mattan because Mattan is his birth father. Mattan knew the reason the Lambs and the Rothledges were told not to mix, and he raped my mother to make that reason happen."

Odelia and Esther both looked like they smelled something foul. "Levana should have said something. We would have ruined Mattan. I'm still going to ruin Mattan. Does Drake know or is Mattan manipulating him? I've never trusted that man."

Odelia already had her phone out. "Drake knows everything, and he's staying with Mattan willingly. If Drake has his attention on Ariel, it means he wants something."

"Excuse me a minute," Odelia said. She didn't even try to leave the room. "Ariel? Get your ass over to the Rothledge Manor immediately. I don't care what Drake says to get you to stay. *Now,* young lady!"

I looked over to the Four Horsemen to see if they could tell anything about Ariel from Odelia. They gave me a curt nod. We'd found the second witness, and maybe Odelia had answers about Lizzie. Or maybe not. Gideon was looking long and hard at Odelia. I had a feeling Gideon was about to say something with his usual impeccable timing and piss Odelia off.

"Levana is not the only one in your circle to have a child in secret that ended up in foster care, is she?" Gideon asked.

Odelia looked shocked. "Who the hell are you? There's no way you could have known that. Only me, Levana, and Esther knew this. Not even the father knew."

"Your child and Levana's were tied together. They ended up in foster care together. Tabitha is not the only prodigal child to return home. Did you feel anything when you met Lizzie?"

Odelia had already started weeping and was looking at Lizzie with cow eyes. I already knew how Lizzie was going to take this and Odelia wasn't going to like it. She was going to have to sit there with her big girl panties on and let Lizzie have her say.

"Lizzie is mine? I felt a pull to her, and I thought she looked familiar. Now that I look at her, without all her makeup, she looks exactly like her father."

Lizzie was livid. I knew that look. She was about to throw some epic shade. "Who knew nothing about me because you ran away to have me, then dumped me in Kentucky. Did you tell Tabby's mom Kentucky was a good place to dump your unwanted kids? Because it's not. The city you sent us to was a total shit hole. There's not even a McDonald's or a Walmart there. Does that tell you something?"

Odelia bowed her head. "You have every right to be angry with me. Maybe I can explain things to both Lizzie and Tabitha. I was sixteen when I fell pregnant with Lizzie. Your father was one of the elders. He was married. I was stupid and thought it was love. When my parents found out, they were the ones who sent me away and arranged the adoption. I argued, but I had almost no say in it. With my parents, they give orders, and you just do it.

"Tabitha, your parents met when they were sixteen too. I knew about your mother's secret romance, and she knew about mine. Your parents started formally petitioning the elders to get married when they were seventeen. They were actually married on your mother's eighteenth birthday. It was about two months after they married that they just stopped seeing people. That must have been after Mattan raped her and they found out about you and Drake.

"It's not an excuse, but we were both so young when we found ourselves pregnant. I don't know how you both ended up in Kentucky. If it had been up to me, I would have kept you. I asked for years what happened to you and I was told you were in a loving home. I don't think Tabitha's parents would have put her in a bad situation intentionally either. Levana wouldn't do that."

Lizzie didn't get a chance to respond. I heard screeching from the foyer. A little pint-sized Goth Lolita came flouncing in. Her skirt was bouncing, and her heels were clacking. She ignored every single person in the room and focused on Odelia.

"Mother, what is it now? Must you hate everyone who's into me? I don't even know if I like Drake yet. He's perfectly nice to me, but there's something about him that I'm trying to figure out if he's dangerous or not."

"Trust me, hon, you can't," Lizzie snapped. She glared at Odelia. "Do you want to tell her or should I?"

Odelia just sighed. "I'll tell her in private. Why do I get the feeling I don't have the whole story here? You wanted Ariel here for a reason. If Ariel and Lizzie are in danger, you'd best tell me now. Ariel will tell you I'm a mama bear and Lizzie will learn."

Bash looked like he found Odelia's anger completely amusing. "Should we tell her, boys?"

"Ariel is seventeen. Don't think because I let her dye her hair or dress a certain way, I'm not going to want to know *exactly* why you all wanted to meet her. I have a feeling there's more to this Drake and Mattan story than you are letting on."

Bash grinned. "Are you sure you want the truth, Mama Bear?"

"I will wipe that smug look off your face no matter how much leather you choose to wear!"

Ariel snorted. Yeah, she was definitely Lizzie's half-sister with that snort. "She means it too."

Lizzie was still pissed, so she just blurted everything out as bluntly as possible. "The reason the Lambs and the Rothledges weren't supposed to mix was that their kid would be the fucking Antichrist. You were so happy and pushing Ariel towards dating him. You win mother of the year again. Tabby is some lion or lamb. Drake tricked her into breaking some seals, and you're actually looking at the Four Horsemen of the Apocalypse. Oh, and I'm a witness, and I'm guessing Ariel is too. Drake is supposed to kill both of us. Still think he's a fucking knight?"

Esther was watching this like a tennis match and nothing Lizzie said seemed even to faze Odelia. She walked over to Zed, who was the biggest of the Four Horsemen. Lizzie must have gotten her height from her father because both Odelia and Ariel were tiny. Odelia barely came up to Zed's armpits, but she poked him in the chest with her finger. Zed looked shocked she would dare.

"Since you're here instead of with Mattan and Drake, does this mean you intend to protect the girls? So help me, if I have to stop this damned apocalypse myself, I'll kill all of you."

Chase and Bash thought it was hilarious all Odelia's rage was focused on Zed until she whirled around and her glare was on them. They both started choking on their laughs and reminded me of fifteen-year-old boys who got caught acting up in class. Gideon was the only one who had control of himself. Gideon pretty much always had control of himself.

"We follow Tabby, not Drake. We're training Lizzie, and we can help Ariel too. Now that we don't have to figure out where Lizzie came from, we can spend more time trying to get into Mattan's security system and trying to figure out his next move. This wasn't supposed to happen yet. Mattan forced it, so we aren't all that motivated to end the world, same as when a child accidentally broke the seals before."

I finally wondered what they got out of this. They were the Four Horsemen of the Apocalypse. What happened to them if the apocalypse didn't happen? I finally asked.

Chase had gotten over his laughter and gave me this sexy elf grin. "Easy. We live out a human life on earth. The seals have accidentally been broken by a child before without the Antichrist being here. We appeared because that's what we do when our seals break. We became playmates and guardians to the child until they were old enough not to need us anymore, but we stayed friends until we died."

Bash winked at me. "Even with the Antichrist here, it's still not the right time. If Tabby, Lizzie, and Ariel stop it this time, our lamb is quite the sexy adult this time. I wouldn't mind sticking around and being a playmate for Tabby."

"Shut up, Bash!" Gideon said sharply.

Gideon was hiding something. Chase and Bash were huge flirts. Even Zed was pretty obvious. They were sly about it and never said anything quite so obvious as that, but there was a reason Lizzie thought I could have my pick over who to blow off some steam with.

Esther finally decided to speak. "Tabitha was in the middle of nowhere in Kentucky. Why wasn't Drake hidden somewhere Mattan couldn't find him?"

I might as well say it. They knew most of the crazy by now and hadn't run. "Drake the cat was really Drake my twin. Mattan snuck in and got the cat and his body. We didn't know if Drake was human again, but apparently, he is. So, thanks for giving us the heads up."

"I could pretend to be into Drake to find out what he's up to. If he's been that cat this entire time, I should be able to manage a twenty-six-year-old virgin," Ariel said, tossing her hair back.

Yeah, she was definitely related to Lizzie.

"Ariel!" Odelia barked. "You can manage boys. You're in over your head with the Antichrist and have you forgotten they said he kills you? Get your ass home. There are things I need to tell you."

Odelia practically dragged Ariel out by her ear. She called over her shoulder to Lizzie she fully intended to have a conversation with her alone the next day. Like me, Lizzie stopped caring who her birth parents were at about fifteen. By that age, we both knew they were never coming to get us, and we'd given up trying to rationalize any reason we'd ended up in our situation. I knew it was going to be rocky for Lizzie and Odelia at first, but after watching Odelia today, she reminded me of Lizzie a little. I knew once Lizzie got over everything, they'd be tight.

Lizzie glared at Gideon. "Did you know Odelia was my mother and I had a sister? Were you just waiting until they got here to dump it like a hot load of shit on me?"

"Actually, no. Any time we were on earth, we've never met any of the witnesses because it wasn't needed. We knew you were a witness right away because you have this glowing light behind your head. Odelia has the same light, and so does Ariel. They are descendants too. Odelia's line must be the witnesses."

"You should talk to her, Lizzie," Chase said. "She was just a scared kid and had no idea where you really ended up. And Ariel sounds like a little firecracker like you."

"Yeah, well, any sister of mine isn't going to fall for sweet talk by a dude who's been a cat for that long and has never talked to a girl before. Her idea of working Drake was a good one if we didn't all know he was going to kill both of us. By the way, if any of you four don't save my sister and me from getting killed, I'm going to haunt you forever. Like, seriously, I'll go poltergeist on your ass."

CHAPTER 16

Ariel pretty much just accepted the apocalypse was happening and she was a witness with a death sentence like we told her it was Tuesday. She was at the house bright an early with a cranky Odelia. Odelia didn't waste time dragging Lizzie away for a little talk. Ariel just flopped on the couch and wanted to talk about my hair. Hers was neon blue, and I thought it looked great on her, but she really wanted purple.

The Four Horsemen just sat there staring at us like we were aliens as I tried to give her tips to get her hair the perfect shade of purple. I knew we needed to be talking about more important things, but this was Lizzie's half-sister and I wanted us to be friends. If that meant ignoring the fact that my brother was intent on ending the world to get her hair just right, the apocalypse could wait five minutes.

Ariel could just flip a switch and change topics like Lizzie. "What does a witness do anyway and why is Drake so interested in me? I'm like jailbait to him anyway. He kept telling my mother he'd respect my age and wait, but I just got this vibe off him there was something wrong with him.

"The creeper vibe," I said, nodding. "Lizzie and I will teach you to hone that skill."

"Can we focus on the apocalypse for a little while?" Gideon asked like he wasn't sure he was going to get yelled yet. He explained the visions and the fire to Ariel like he had done with Lizzie.

Gideon went through the same meditation and breathing exercises as he had with Lizzie. Ariel was in deep concentration until we all jumped up because we heard Odelia screaming. I hoped Lizzie hadn't punched her. Lizzie was a hothead, and I'd watched her punch plenty of guys, but she wouldn't deck her own mother, right?

We all went running, and I smelled smoke. Lizzie and Odelia were in the library furiously trying to put out a desk that was engulfed in flames. Jana ran in with a fire extinguisher and finally got it out. It didn't ruin the hardwood floors, but that rug was going to have to go.

Odelia was in a panic and Lizzie seemed excited. Jana was fussing about smoking in the house. We just let her think someone had lit up and promised not to do it again. Gideon walked over and grabbed Lizzie's shoulders.

"You did this. The flame had a blue tinge to it. How did you manage to produce the fire and where did it come from?"

"We were fighting, and it came out her mouth! If the desk hadn't been there, she would have set *me* on fire!" Odelia yelled.

"Pretty badass, right? I wasn't trying to set *you* on fire. It was an accident. I was getting angry, and I felt this burning in my stomach. The next thing I know, I turned into Smaug the dragon!"

"We'll have to work on your aim and how to control it, but this is excellent progress, Lizzie!" Chase said, swooping her up in a huge hug.

"Outside without relatives in the way. There are antiques in this house," Odelia said. She seemed to have forgiven Lizzie for nearly torching her. "Will this protect Lizzie and Ariel from Drake?"

All four Horsemen were grinning. "Now, that we know the fire comes from their mouth and not from their hands, we know why Drake wants them dead. The texts are vague about the witnesses. Some have interpreted them as trees or lampposts that produce fire. Lizzie and Ariel may have the ability to knock Drake back into the pits of hell," Zed said.

"Drake wouldn't know this. He would know about the fire and the prophecy, but he wouldn't know the theories it would be gifted to kill him. Drake was probably interested in Lizzie and

Ariel because he hoped to use their gift of prophecy for his own gain, then kill them when he didn't need them, or they turned on him."

Even though Lizzie nearly set Odelia on fire, whatever she said to her seemed to have Lizzie in a better mood. She slung her arm around Ariel's shoulder and tossed her hair back.

"He also could have been interested in us because we're both hot as fuck. He wouldn't know what to do with either of us anyway."

Odelia groaned. "Lizzie, please keep in mind your sister is only seventeen. Even with being able to blow the Antichrist straight to hell, she's still a minor."

I think everyone in the room just ignored her. Ariel squealed and hugged Lizzie. "Does this mean you're moving in with us and taking our last name? Can we share clothes? That skirt you were wearing yesterday was amazing."

"Come on, runt, that skirt would go down to your ankles. What *is* our last name anyway? I hate the one they gave me in the foster system."

Whoever decided to stick Lizzie with the last name Feltersnatch was just setting her up for a whole string of stupid nicknames. Mine wasn't much better at Horr. We used to joke they did it on purpose just to torture us. I had a feeling whatever came out of Ariel or Odelia's mouth was going to be Lizzie's new last name unless it was somehow worse than Feltersnatch.

"Lizzie Belcourt has a nice ring to it if you chose to use our last name," Odelia said. She said it like she desperately wanted Lizzie to take her last name.

"Lizzie Belcourt it is then. Come on, runt. Let's go outside and see what your trigger is for fire too. Gideon, come with us."

I thought Lizzie would understand me not going out there with them and possibly getting set on fire. I went back inside with Bash, Chase, and Zed. They didn't' seem to want to be set on fire either. Or, maybe they just wanted to spend more time with me. I liked that idea better.

Chase went straight to his laptop. Bash grabbed me and hauled me into his lap. I wanted to fight him, but as soon as he wrapped his arms around me and I was pressed against his chest, I realized Bash didn't just have a sexy voice. He smelled like pure sex too. I heard him chuckle when I groaned and just leaned back into his chest. Normally, I could resist anyone, but every single one of the Horsemen made my body tingle.

"Are you two trying to kill me?" I asked when Zed grabbed my feet again and started rubbing them.

I was like this limp little noodle in a pile of leather, muscle, and sex. Zed gave me this evil little grin and worked his thumbs in the ball of my feet. He knew exactly what he was doing to me.

"What do you think, Bash? Think we can get her to whimper and beg?"

"What the fuck? I'll kill you."

I said that like a total wimp. I might as well have been whimpering. I said it dreamily and with no conviction at all. Now, Chase was laughing. He'd better not be laughing at me because he wasn't the one sending me some weird Horsemen pheromones. That's what this was. They were sending some weird cosmic shit at me. I wasn't getting up though. This was nice as hell.

"We can all make her beg later. I've gotten into Mattan's security system. To use a Tabby and Lizzie word, the man's a creeper. He's got nanny cams in the maid's room. His maids live in the house. He's got cams in the showers."

"Ew! Zed, have you figured out his punishment yet?"

"Not yet. It has to be just right. But this gives me ammo. Do we know what Drake and Mattan are up to?"

"I have a feeling they are meeting in a secret room with no camera, but…wait for it. He uses the same password for everything. I can get into his computer."

"I could kiss all of you," I purred.

Bash's cologne was overwhelming me. It was probably called something like *Epic Sex Magic* because that was how it made me feel. Zed had moved from my feet and was massaging my calves. Chase was getting into Mattan's fortress. Yeah, I definitely wanted to fuck all of them, even Gideon, who wasn't here. They'd said things along the lines they'd be up for it too and they'd been flirting this entire time.

Could the lamb have a group thing with the Four Horsemen? Asking for a friend.

CHAPTER 17

It had been a long day, but I couldn't sleep. Chase was still trying to get past all of Mattan's firewalls, but Lizzie and Ariel were apparently getting really good with their fire. Lizzie hated smoking, but she decided to do parlor tricks and show me how she could blow smoke rings out her mouth now. I warned her if she set anything in the house on fire, I was going to start calling her the Dragon Lady. That was what we called our foster mother the first time we met. She was a chain smoker and spent all the money she was supposed to spend on us on Marlboro Reds.

I should have been passed out, but I couldn't sleep. It was Gideon's turn to guard me. The rest of the Horsemen took the rest of the house, and someone would sit with me while I slept. Gideon always sat on a chaise across the room from my bed, and his eyes never left my bed. My bed gave him an eye on the door. I felt safe with all of them watching me. Gideon always had his sword with him across his lap.

I missed snuggling with Bash and Chase and Zed's massages. Gideon never touched me, but he was always staring at me. I couldn't sleep, and I wanted to know what Gideon's touch felt like. I wanted to know if he smelled as soon as the others. Bash smelled like straight up sex, Chase smelled like burning leaves, sandalwood, and musk, and Zed smelled like citrus.

I padded out of bed and walked over to the chaise Gideon was sitting on. For once, he didn't stare at me; he stared at my feet.

"What is it, Tabby? I prefer you under the covers when you sleep in clothes like that."

"I can't sleep," I said, feeling unsure of myself for once. Now that he commented on my sleeping apparel, which was just an old tank top and some tiny shorts, I felt bad about wanting to sit in his lap and having him hold me.

Gideon's eyes started on my toes and trailed up my body until they met mine. I could have sworn his green eyes were glowing, but they actually seemed to soften a little in the darkness. He set his sword aside.

"Would you feel better if I played with your hair?"

"Only Lizzie has before."

"No boyfriends?" he asked, patting the seat next to him.

I laid down and rested my head on his lap. "I've never met a guy I wanted to get serious with before. No serious boyfriends. I've had booty calls and fuck buddies, and some of them got attached, but I ended it."

"You don't want to fall in love, Tabitha?"

I thought I didn't. I thought I was fine with just getting my rocks off. Maybe all the boys I'd met still had cooties until I met the Four Horsemen. Now that I knew if we stopped Drake, they would be staying, I wanted to keep them. They were hot as hell and managed to be funny, sweet, and sarcastic at the same time.

I closed my eyes when his hands started running through my hair. This was nice. Different than with Lizzie. I swear I was about to start purring like Drake did when he was a cat.

"Don't get attached to us, Tabitha. I know how everyone acts around you, but they know what is going to happen."

My eyes flew open. "How about you tell *me* what is going to happen? Did something happen with the other Lambs?"

"Not the other Lambs. They were all children, and we only ever looked at them like sisters. We come into the world almost at the same time, and it's like we're connected. We *always* fall for the same woman. We are connected when it comes to things hurting us and dying. What always happened was that the woman would pick one of us and the other three would die of the broken heart. That would kill the one chosen too."

I bit my lip. That was certainly rough, and I didn't want to kill any of them just because I wanted to get in their pants. And I was starting to feel like I wanted more than just getting in their pants for all of them. I knew part of that was because I never had anyone wanting to protect me before. I was probably just projecting my issues on them, and I'd end up killing them.

Gideon's thumb traced my lower lip, and I shivered. I'd done more than my share of a freak show in the bedroom, but that had to be one of the most erotic things anyone had done to me, and I had all my clothes on.

"None of us know if we all just have the same taste and it never ends well, or there's something cosmic about it. We aren't technically supposed to be on earth, and there's not much that can kill us, so a broken heart does it. The other three need to learn to behave around you. *I* shouldn't be doing this now."

I bit his thumb, and he groaned. I could feel his erection growing where my head was rested in his lap. "This isn't the dark ages, or whenever it was, you were last here. Different relationships are being recognized now. What if you had a woman that was into all four of you and saw you as different men?"

"That's not human nature—"

"Says who? There are entire porn channels for that now. Those are actually my favorite."

Gideon let out a little growl and he pulled my hair a bit. So, finally I found something that got him riled up. "Tabby, I don't think the apocalypse, the Four Horsemen, the Antichrist, or Satan was quite prepared for *you*. I'll admit, we've never met an adult Lamb yet and the ones we did know, we met as children and guided into adults. You're quite the naughty little minx even without all the leather and tattoos."

I nipped at his thumb again since I knew it turned him on. Riled up Gideon was my new favorite Gideon. That bulge under my head was promising, and he was panting like any minute, he was going to rip my clothes off and fuck the shit out of me. God, that would be so hot. If it sent the rest of them running to my room, I was all up for a fivesome.

"The four of you are ones to talk with all the leather you wear."

"Yes, but none of us quite have bodies like you do," he panted pulling my hair again.

Damn it, if he wasn't going to make a move, I was. I wrestled myself into a sitting position and straddled his lap. "None of you have bodies like I do?" I teased, grinding against his erection. My shorts were thin and already sticking to me I was so wet. "The four of you have bodies that would make any girl sin. I'm shocked anyone in history was able to pick just one of you. You're all fucking gorgeous, and none of you make me want to stick my boot up your ass."

Gideon didn't stop me. He rested his head on the back of the chaise and squeezed my ass. "You and those boots, Tabby. I'd take one up the ass just to get you to take them off. Do you wear those around the house to torture us?"

"Oh, I think all of you are doing a little torturing of your own when it comes to me, don't you, Gideon?" I asked, grinding into him a little harder.

Jesus fuck, I was about to come just from doing this and that had never happened to me before. I hadn't even kissed him yet. I hadn't kissed any of them. If I got to fuck them, I'd probably turn into a pile of goo.

Gideon's head snapped up. "I can't make love to you tonight, Tabitha. I can tell you're close. Use my body and come, love."

I was clutching his shoulders for dear life. I wanted more. If I couldn't have him, I wanted more. "Will you at least kiss me?" I gasped.

Gideon moved like lightning. He didn't just kiss me; he consumed me. I'd never been kissed like that in my entire life. It was passionate, raw, and primal. Gideon bit my lower lip, and I came undone. I bit him back and rode out my orgasm. I buried my face in his neck. Gideon smelled good too. He smelled like lavender. When I finally calmed down, I started laughing.

I pulled back and looked him in the eye. "Is that some special skill you get as a Horseman of the Apocalypse? Make a girl come that hard when neither of you is naked with just a little bite."

"Ah, Tabby. I lost control and shouldn't have done that. Tomorrow, it's going to be game on with the others. You just think they were flirting with you before. And seeing as what happens to us when you do pick, none of us is going to give you what you want," he said, tracing my bottom lip with his thumb again.

Gideon seemed under the impression I was going to choose eventually and they were going to die. No, now that I knew what was going to happen, I wasn't picking. I had three jobs now. Stop the apocalypse, destroy Drake, and convince all four of them we needed to have some sort of polyamorous kink thing going on.

My mind was already spinning with fantasies.

100

Chapter 18

Part of the reason I was having so much trouble sleeping the night before was that Lizzie wasn't with me. She'd almost instantly bonded with Ariel learning to blow smoke like a dragon and decided to spend the night at her mother's house. I knew she wouldn't move in there permanently. Lizzie would stay there a good while getting to know everyone, but I don't think Lizzie's mouth could form the words she still lived at home and she'd want her own space. If it weren't with me, she'd be close by.

Lizzie wasn't there when I went down for breakfast, but four smirking Horsemen were sitting at the table eating eggs.

"Tabby, you know I'm Conquest, right? Couldn't you get the urge to fool around with me first? Gideon wasn't even trying!" Chase said, winking at me. I knew he wasn't mad, but he wanted his turn.

"My fingers aren't just good at rubbing your feet," Zed said waggling his eyebrows.

"If just holding you in my lap does that to you, you should see what I can do with my tongue," Bash said, winking at me.

I cocked an eyebrow at all of them. Gideon was with me all night. He slept in bed with me after a lot of convincing. He didn't have time to get all chatty about what we did.

"Can you talk to each other in your heads like Drake did with me when he was in the cat? Can Drake still do that?"

I was shocked Gideon kissed my knuckles in front of the others. "I tried to warn you last night. We can talk telepathically, but we never do about this. It's part of what happens when the woman we love chooses and why I told you we shouldn't. They can *feel* it. And Drake can talk telepathically. I'm shocked he hasn't tried by now. If he hasn't, he's plotting something."

I'd deal with Drake in a minute. They'd all thrown down some sort of gauntlet knowing what was going to happen if I chose before we'd dealt with Drake. I already knew I didn't want to pick. I had this huge fantasy in my head about playing house with the Four Horsemen of the Apocalypse. They all brought something I liked to the table.

I threw down my own gauntlet. "So, before Lizzie gets here and we start dealing with our Drake problem, why don't we go do everything you just suggested? *Together."*

I'd finally found something to shock these four huge warriors. Oddly, they didn't fight or get jealous. They were shocked I'd suggested that in the first place and it had rendered them all speechless. We all just sat there in silence. I issued the challenge. It was a solution for them being able to live out full human lives with no hurt.

It seemed like endless silence. It looked like they were actually figuring out if I was serious or this was actually possible. They didn't have time to say anything because Lizzie, Ariel, Odelia, and Esther came in with a girl I didn't recognize. It had to be Esther's daughter Natalia because I already knew she dressed like me from Esther. Not *exactly,* but she had a fondness for black leather and black eyeliner. Natalia was tall and wasn't owning it in a good pair of fuck me boots.

And Lizzie! What the hell happened to Lizzie? Lizzie gravitated towards blonde college girls going through their experimental phase who were just using her. It was always the same — some preppy blonde girl with huge boobs who treated her like shit.

Natalia wasn't blonde. Her hair was dyed black, and Lizzie never went for the whole goth look before. Natalia wasn't seventeen like Ariel. Natalia looked like she was my age. And Lizzie looked like she was super into Natalia. Did breathing fire totally change her taste in girls? Screw the Horsemen and their inability to talk at my suggestion for group sex. I needed to talk to my best friend.

"Can I borrow Lizzie? If you're all done eating, you should get to work trying to figure out Mattan's plans."

Esther just smiled at me. "I've already figured out some of Mattan's plans. We're going to have visitors here later. Now, I suggest you go talk to Lizzie and come back soon."

Esther looked like she saw through both of us. I wondered if my mother were still with us, I'd not be able to get away with anything with her. It kind of hit me right then I'd never know that because Drake killed her. Probably to set things in motion to get me here. After I talked to Lizzie, the first thing on my agenda was figuring out how to kill Drake without hurting Lizzie or Ariel.

As soon as we were alone, Lizzie wasn't herself. She squealed and grabbed my arm. Lizzie just did not get that excited about anything.

"Isn't Natalia amazing? Esther stayed over with us and brought her. I didn't go to bed until six this morning because we were up late just talking. She's perfect."

"Yeah, but she's just so different than anyone I've seen you go after before."

Lizzie shrugged and told me something I apparently hadn't figured out on my own yet. "Those were revenge fucks. All those girls who thought they were using me to go through their little bisexual phase, I was using them. That is the exact kind of girl that tortured me in middle school. Then, they think they meet a desperate lesbian willing to put up with their shit while they figure things out. I made all of them beg for it. They were the ones dependent on me. When they decided they were going back to dudes, it was no sweat off my back. *But* when their new boyfriends were going down on them, they were always going to remember how good I was at it and they screamed my name and begged me."

"It sounds like you want to get serious with Natalia. What changed?"

Lizzie just squeezed me. "Literally, everything. Odelia is actually amazing when you get to know her. I don't blame her for what happened to me. My little runt of a sister is a badass with that flame we have. I ended up in the same foster home as you for a reason. You're my sister too. I have a purpose now.

Me, you, and my real family, we're ending the fucking apocalypse and stopping the Antichrist. I thought we were going to spend the rest of our lives serving drinks at that bar until our tits started sagging and no one would tip us, then we'd have to go be phone sex operators or something."

"I've made a decision about relationships too. I want one with all four of the Horsemen. Don't you think it would be awesome to live in this house with all four of them?"

Lizzie threw back her head and laughed. "Well, aren't you just a greedy little bitch. How do they feel about that?"

"Total silence when I bought it up. Gideon gave me a mind-blowing orgasm with both our clothes on without even touching me."

"Do they have some sort of psychic penis that's better than a vibrator?"

"No, Lizzie. I'll give you more details later. Right now, we need to worry about Drake. You've got the fire down, anything with the prophecy?"

"Oh, yeah, I forgot to tell you. Ariel and I are better at that together. It's what Esther meant about guests. We think Drake hasn't made his move yet because Mattan is preparing him. Drake needs acolytes. He's going to go for the elders and the thirteen families first. He already started by getting Odelia over there with Ariel. That was a grab at the runt, but if he had Odelia's ear, he hoped she would turn the other families against you. He underestimated my mother. She went directly to you to call you out to your face instead of gossiping behind your back."

"She's definitely your mother then. Is my new house going to be full of strange people?"

I never did well in crowds. Working at a bar was miserable if there was a football game on. That would be nothing compared to thirteen families consisting of who knows how many people in my house wanting me to tell my story. I didn't do well with public speaking either. I totally froze, and I even puked once.

"Tabby, come on. Who are you talking to? Only the elders are coming. And we should get out there because Esther invited them in about an hour. Just to warn you, your grandparents are going to be there. Mattan just told everyone you were a distant heir. That was why none of the elders were at the welcome home party. They are very interested in you now."

There was a knock at the door. When I opened it, it was Natalia, and she looked like she was hoping Lizzie would answer. I grinned to myself. I could tell Natalia dug her too. If she hurt my friend, I'd break her face, but right now, it looked like she wanted to get to know her better. I was grinning like a total shit head as I walked behind them and I watched Natalia tentatively slip her hand into Lizzie's. I tried not to squeal like a pig because I'd wanted Lizzie with someone who would make her happy for the longest time.

When I followed them out to the sitting area, it was full of people. Two older couples approached me. The woman of one of them looked like my mother, and the man from the other looked like Elliot. They all looked like they were about to burst into tears and they all took turns hugging me — real hugs that kind of hurt a little.

The couple that I could tell was Elliot's parents smiled at me gently. "We don't care what Mattan did. You're still our grandchild. You still have Lamb blood. We hope you'll call us Nona and Sabba."

"Of course," I said, hugging them both again. I did have real family here.

My mother's family came over to me next. My grandmother stroked my cheek. "I think Levana would like your look. She was always into playing dress up. Will you call us Oma and Opa?"

Now, I was the one bawling like an asshole. My grandparents led me over to the sofa and made a fortress around me. My Nona was stroking my hair, and my Oma was stroking my cheek. Sabba and Opa were on either side of them holding them. We were a unit — a *family.* And Mattan and Drake weren't going to tear us apart. I was going to fight for them.

When I was reduced to a sniveling mess, someone across the room cleared their throat. "This could have waited until after you'd met your family. Should we leave?" a severe looking man said.

"No. We need to deal with Drake and Mattan," I said, wiping my eyes. Oma squeezed my arm.

"So, we've got the Lamb, the Antichrist, the Horsemen, and the two witnesses are already coming into their gifts?"

"I'm sorry, I don't know you," Lizzie snapped. I didn't either. I didn't know any of them.

"Herschel Hutchrance. I'm sort of what you would call a leader out of the group. I've never trusted the Adlers. Irina, when Levana and Elliot went to get married, you came to me about the Adlers. I didn't hear you out then, and I'm sorry. Tell me what you wanted to tell me then."

Well, I knew where Lizzie got it from now, and I was starting to see what I got it from. My Oma glared at Herschel. "You mean when I told you about the conditions? We all had to fight with Opal when we were negotiating for Elliot and Levana to marry. Opal didn't want the two of them together. She kept suggesting a union with Levana and Mattan instead. Like Elliot and Levana weren't totally smitten with each other! Knowing what you know now, can you see why?"

"Aren't there elders from all families?" I asked. "Isn't someone with Mattan's family here?"

Herschel grinned at me. "No, dear. When we found out someone in the Adler family had committed rape and started the apocalypse, we met without them. I had no idea if it was just Mattan or the entire family. It sounds like if what Irina says is true, it's the entire family."

"Then why wait until now to do it?" I asked.

"Opportunity," Ariel said. "If an Adler just raped a female Rothledge, then they would be punished and not given the opportunity to guide the child. When Elliot and Levana got together, it gave them the window. When the condition was given to get a vasectomy, they knew if Levana ended up pregnant and tried to blame Mattan, they could just say she was blaming Mattan to cover up her mistakes."

Lizzie was grinning proudly at Ariel, and I was pretty damned impressed with the runt too. Herschel was grinning at her.

"I want to know how Lizzie and I both ended up in Kentucky," I demanded. "It doesn't make sense that out of the entire world, we both wind up in the middle of nowhere in the same place."

A tiny, older lady cleared her throat. "I can answer that. You may call me Sara. There was an orphanage in Kentucky, and it's kind of like our dirty little secret. Many children from the families end up there. We didn't know about you and Lizzie, but all of the families know about it to send children to. It was founded by one of the family members a long time ago. We had no idea it had come to such a state it's in now that you and Lizzie went through what you did. I'm going to have a talk with them and remove all our financial backing unless they straighten up.

"Yes, girl, they were given a lot of money to make sure children found good homes. They apparently pocketed it and didn't do the right thing. I've half a mind to sue them."

"You'll have to find a different lawyer if Mattan handles all your law work," I snorted.

"Actually, *I* handle all the law work," a tall man said. "My name is Arlen. I'm handling a huge case right now for all the families, and Mattan asked to handle your family's estate. Trust me; if Sara says to sue, they won't be left with a penny to their name *and* all the children will find homes."

"You're not going to be able to any of that unless you stop Drake," Ariel reminded them.

"Well, we've got the witnesses, the lamb, and the Four Horsemen here," Herschel said. "I think we can come up with a plan."

My Four Horsemen were oddly quiet, like they wanted us to figure this out on our own. I needed to think. What would the Antichrist do in this century?

"He's going to need followers, right?" I asked. "That was the whole point of getting to you. He would start with the elders and use your resources to get more." Nona and Oma both squeezed my hand like I was on the right track.

"It won't be long before he figures out the elders are on our side," Lizzie said. "It may make him careless."

"It will," Ariel said. "He knows it's going to be harder to get to Tabby to get her to break the other seals. And she can't break them before he's ready. He tricked her into breaking the first four because he hoped the Four Horsemen would help him. Tabby would feel sorry for him and be on his side."

Lizzie snorted. "Because he didn't do his research on Tabby. He's going to need to start building a following now. How he's going to do that now is social media. Twitter, Instagram, YouTube. He's probably already started. One of you big, beefy Horsemen with computer skills hasn't found that yet?"

Chase and Gideon already had their computers out. Gideon was silently typing away, and Chase was muttering about how you were supposed to get anything said with meaning with a limited number of characters. They both looked up at the same time like they found something. Gideon actually grinned.

"If Tabby or Lizzie sees this, they are going to smash my laptop. I've got a feeling the little witness is going to as well."

"What?" I demanded.

"Our laptops are top of the line, and we're going to need them in the future, Tabby," Chase said. He had this shit eating grin on his face like Drake was building an army of evil clowns or something. I don't care how harmless or goofy they seemed; clowns freaked me out. It was probably a good thing we didn't have a McDonalds back in Kentucky.

Zed and Bash had both gotten up to look over Chase and Gideon's shoulders.

"Incels?" Bash scoffed. "The Antichrist is an Incel, and *that* is who he is building a following of?"

Lizzie let out her famous snort. "*Of course,* he's a fucking Incel. Right after he gets let out of being a cat, one of the girls he's into plots to kill him and the other one who is actually illegal runs away. He probably thinks all you Horsemen are Chads stealing his women. He'd better be referring to the runt and me as Stacys and not Beckys."

Lizzie served drinks to a guy who kept insulting her and calling her Stacy all night. He kept calling the other bartender Chad and insinuating Lizzie and the other bartender were fucking in the alley on breaks. It ended up being the bouncer that overheard and dropped the term *Incel* to Lizzie right before booting the dude on his ass once his taunts got worse the more he drank. Lizzie was obsessed after that and read everything she could about it.

Herschel was looking at her like she was insane. "Care to explain that to the rest of the room? And keep in mind most of us are in our seventies and don't visit online forums."

I just nodded to Lizzie. She could have written a fucking dissertation on Incels. She stood and ran her hands down her skirt. She put her hands behind her back, and I could tell this was going to be some huge, dramatic Lizzie speech. If she could have tucked a pencil behind her ear like a television college professor, she would have.

"Okay, so, Incels. Listen up. Incel means involuntary celibate. They are a bunch of pale little white boys sitting in their momma's basements posting on forums about how the government should mandate programs so that women should *have* to fuck them. Like, they think it's their god given right to get sex from women, and some of them want the governments to help. They get pretty rapey and think if the government won't help them, they make all these plots on how to rape and get away with it.

"There's all this slang with the Incels, and they hate people who are actually going out and getting laid. Like, they want us girls to fuck them, but they don't actually want us fucking anyone else. Guys that are actually getting fucked are called Chads. Hot girls getting laid are called Stacys. Less hot girls getting fucked are called Beckys. They want the Stacys and the Beckys to fuck them, but they are sluts for having a good time with anyone else that doesn't give off creeper momma's basement vibes like an Incel."

Odelia cleared her throat. "That you for that explanation, dear."

"Whatever happened to using a sock and your imagination until you managed to properly romance a bird?" my Opa said. Okay, clearly, I didn't just inherit my mouth from the females in the family. My Opa was a badass too.

"Do the four of you want to stay for dinner?" I asked. I wanted to get to know all of them so badly.

Nona just smiled at me gently. "Of course, but I believe your friend just gave us a little lesson about the kind of men your brother will recruit. We need to worry about that."

Sara just threw back her head and let out a laugh. She kind of reminded me of like, this really evil Yoda right at that minute, but I had a feeling whatever she was going to say was going to ruin Drake's plans. Everyone in the room had to be an elder for a reason. None of them had said a word to me about my twin being the Antichrist or how I wasn't supposed to be born. They were all being *nice* to me, and they wanted to help me. That was something new for me, and I kind of liked it.

"Mattan's wife has complained to the elders a few times about Mattan. Nothing we had the power to do anything about, but there's a particular escort service he likes to use. I would imagine he's bringing women for Drake now that he's not a cat and he didn't get the women he wanted. What would this sad little community of perverts do with a video reel of Drake with a bunch of different beautiful women?"

Lizzie crossed her arms. It was a good idea, but she was thinking the same thing I was.

"Only if you can blur out the women's faces," I said. "I don't want any of them getting hurt, and whatever is filmed and released, it's not actually them having sex. I don't care how old you are; I think everyone here would agree you wouldn't want a video of you fucking anyone on the internet."

Finally, the Horsemen decided to contribute something. They had all been hunched over the laptops, and I thought they weren't paying attention. They weren't looking at the elders now. They were looking at me. I remembered them telling me they answered to me. How the hell did I go from not know if I was going to make rent to having the Four Horsemen of the Apocalypse at my beck and call?

"Tabby, we knew about the escort service. There have been women at the house ever since Ariel stopped talking to Drake. I guess he didn't care she was only seventeen. There's a camera at the door, and Drake is the one that answers," Gideon said. "He's pretty much panting like a hungry puppy. The Incel stuff was started probably right after he became human again and found out Lizzie wasn't going to be his first. He must have decided to stick with it, even with the escorts coming in and out, because he seems to have fans."

"Great, we've got to stop the Antichrist and his army of perverts who are angry about not getting laid," I muttered.

Sara was still staring at me. "You surprise me, Tabitha. You grew up totally away from here, but you take after everyone in your family *except* your Adler blood. None of the Adlers would have had any issues releasing videos of Drake having sex with those women. How did you want to play this without doing that?"

I lifted my chin stubbornly. She was the first person to mention Mattan was my father today. She didn't do it in a bad way, but I wasn't sure I wanted to just blindly follow someone who was okay with ruining women's lives like that. Sure, we would be stopping the end of the world, but I'd worked in strip clubs before. Some of those women visiting Drake and Matten could have the exact same story as the women who danced. Really, people looked down on strippers and sex workers, but a lot of the women and men doing it were the ones with all the power. People came from miles around just to throw money at you to see you without your clothes on or pay you for sex. You were the one getting rich in that situation.

"I'm using my resources before I make a plan. I've got two witnesses, Four Horsemen, and now all the elders here. Drake is cunning, even if he technically never left the house as a cat. Mattan has probably been planning this for years. We can't make any stupid moves. If we do something, it needs to be after it's been gone over with a fine-tooth comb."

Lizzie had my back like always. Apparently, so did Ariel. I was starting to like that kid. "We don't release sex tapes," Lizzie said. "There's got to be a way to show Drake's got beautiful women around him whenever he wants without ruining other lives besides Drake and Mattan's."

"I get the feeling Drake is going to react worse to that than to us taking the elders away," Ariel said. "The elders have a bigger reach as far as money and tech, but I get the feeling he identifies with the Incels more. I have this feeling Drake is going to make a huge move when those videos are released," Ariel said.

"I have the same feeling as the runt," Lizzie said.

"Good," I said, nodding. "I want Drake shaken up and careless. This is what's going to happen. I don't even know if we could have gotten cameras in the bedroom in the first place—"

"Um, Tabby?" Chase said. "There are cameras in there. Drake gets off on the reruns."

"Gross, Chase. So, this is the plan. We can take the footage of Drake letting the women into the house, then again to his bedroom. If Drake makes an ass of himself *before* the woman gets naked, we'll make a copy of that. Let Drake build an army of Incels for now. We'll be recording him and expose him as a false prophet to the Incels. Take away Drake's merry band of perverts and Drake is going to leave Mattan's fortress to face me. I'll be ready and so will the witnesses and the Horsemen."

CHAPTER 19

I was barely walking on two feet when I went to bed. I totally understood what Lizzie was feeling now and why she was spending so much time at the Belcourt Manor with her mother and sister. My grandparents were *amazing*. Elliot's parents were still distant relatives of mine through the Lamb connection to the Adlers, but we just ignored that. We pretended Elliot was my birth father and I called them Nona and Sabba. Somehow, I was just guessing my grandparents from Mattan were just as horrible as he was.

All four of them were amazing. They told me stories of my parents when they were growing up. Elliot was pretty straight-laced and my mother liked to get in trouble like me. Apparently, Elliot had been in love with her since kindergarten and she totally friend zoned him until they were fourteen and Elliot hit his growth spurt. She hadn't even realized he was smitten with her and started hitting on him pretty hard, which just confused the hell out of him.

Both my grandparents were joking about how it was this awkward mess of hormones and miscommunication for a while before they both finally figured out they were into each other. Then, they could joke about it and were inseparable. The story of my parent's romance, both how they ended up together and afterwards, dominated dinner. It was sweet and totally not like me to get all mushy-eyed about a romance story. That was a genre I normally stayed away from. Maybe I was turning into a mutant since I got here.

Mutant or not, I threw a gauntlet down this morning and so did my Horsemen. Zed was guarding me tonight, and I believe he made a promise about his fingers over breakfast. I just got this vibe none of them were going to give me what I wanted and fuck me unless I could convince them to do it all together, so I didn't kill them. What I didn't get was why they were flirting so hard if my vagina was a death sentence for all of them.

I opened my bedroom door and stopped dead in my tracks. I guess Zed was intending on keeping his promise. He was sprawled out on my bed wearing leather trousers and nothing else. I gaped like a total virgin for a minute because Zed didn't look like the Horseman of Justice. His dark skin contrasted with the cream-colored sheets. He had his hands behind his head and was just grinning at me.

I'd seen Bash in his vests, but I'd never seen any of them without their shirts on before. My eyes took in his perfectly sculpted chest and abs, then looked V his hip muscles made as they disappeared into those leather trousers. I finally stopped gawking like a virgin at her first strip show.

"Are you going to keep those trousers on?"

Zed just chuckled. "You're the first adult Lamb we've encountered so far. This is all quite new to us. I don't think any of us were expecting to be so attracted to you, nor what you suggested this morning."

I ran to the bed and dove in with him. I snuggled my face into his hard chest. "I was totally serious by the way. I want all four of you."

"And that got all of our attention, but we think you'll eventually prefer one of us over the other."

My hand started playing with his washboard abs. "I totally won't. I can't even pick a favorite food or television show."

Zed chuckled. "Please, you go apeshit over waffles. Waffles is your favorite food."

"I've gone apeshit over everything I've been served since I got here. Waffles is just *one* of my favorite foods. Steak is good. So is pizza. The lamb we had for dinner two nights ago was fucking amazing. Nachos are awesome. I didn't think I'd like sushi, but Jana convinced me to try it, and now I want more."

"You're all over the place; you know that? Sometimes, I can't keep up."

"It's easy, Zed," I said, biting his chest. "I like what I like when I like it, and I don't want to be pinned down into choosing anything. I like all four of you. You all bring different things to the table. I've thought about this. I've never bothered with anyone to have a serious relationship. I want to do that with *all* of you."

"You do manage to talk a lot of sense, Tabby. You say things that make me forget all my previous lives on Earth. You make me think what you want could actually work."

"The four of you don't get all jealous and just use your Horsemen gifts against each other? It's weird that you die of a broken heart instead of just like, murdering each other. I don't get jealous because I don't date and apparently Lizzie has been on a revenge fuck streak, but I would imagine no matter how close we are, if I were a lesbian and looked at Natalia the wrong way, she'd think up some pretty epic way of killing me."

"Actually, no. We're all brothers in some way, created for the same thing. We can feel each other no matter what we do. I could feel Gideon getting all hot and bothered the night before. It doesn't turn us on or anything; we can just sense things. We've *always* fallen for the same woman — every single time. I don't know if it's because one of us does and we all feel it and fall in love with her because one of us does, or it's because we just have similar tastes.

"But you're all so different. You don't even have the same tastes in food."

Zed found that hilarious. "Little lamb, you've only been around us a few days. You think you know our preferences in food?"

"Sure. Every time Jana serves waffles, Gideon has his with blueberries, Chase does strawberries and whipped cream, Bash does bananas and chocolate, and you are a total waffle freak. You do chocolate hazelnut spread, maple syrup, chocolate syrup, *and* whipped cream. Gideon likes his food clean. Lean meats and minimal sauce. Chase kind of strikes me as someone who'd go vegetarian if the three of you wouldn't give him shit about it. Bash is a total foodie. He likes everything fatty with rich sauces. And you, Mister Justice. When you think we're not looking, you look up fast food menus for you to eat at when the apocalypse is over. You know they have delivery apps, and you can just have someone bring it here?"

Zed rolled me on my back and started stroking my cheeks. "How did you notice all that in just a few days? You're making me think what you want is actually possible. I'll talk the others into trying it, okay? I believe I promised to show you what my fingers could do. If you show me that delivery app so I can get Taco Bell, I'll pull out every single trick I know and make your eyes roll back in your head."

"I'll tell you the best thing to order if you let me reciprocate."

Zed started nibbling on my neck. "How about you tell me the most delicious, worst for you, thing on the menu and you'll owe me one if I can convince the others?"

"Since when are you the bossy one?"

"Tabby, I'm *quite* bossy in bed. You've never had me in your bed before. I'm glad you wore a skirt today," he purred, running his tongue down my neck. "I can get you naked and leave those boots that drive us all crazy on."

I lucked out more than I knew with these boots. I randomly found them on a trip to Goodwill, and they happened to fit. I'd been tipped well the night before, and they were only five dollars. They were black leather and went above my knee with a six-inch heel and platform. I was six feet tall in these boots, and they made me feel like a total badass. They were comfortable as hell too. I'd been wearing them all the time now because the Horsemen loved checking out my legs when I was wearing them.

"Are you a dominant, kinky fuck, Zed?" I asked. I hoped he was. I *really* hoped he was.

He answered by biting me. "This is the perfect headboard for me to tie you down. I think I'll do it with this spiked belt of yours."

He had my belt unbuckled and yanked it off in one hard pull. If Zed wanted to be dominant, I could be submissive. I wasn't a dom or a sub. I was what I was in the mood for when I was playing with someone. Zed never struck me as being bossy at all, but if he was into that in bed, I already knew I was going to have fun.

I let him undress me. I was totally naked except for my boots. Zed growled and looked down at me. He adjusted his erection and grabbed my belt. I grabbed the slats on the headboard because I thought that was what he wanted, but he grabbed my hands and put them on my stomach. He wagged his finger at me like I was being naughty.

"I promised you tricks. You should wait until you are told to do something."

"What should I call you?" Some guys I'd been with liked *Master* or *Sir* if we were playing this game. Personally, I hated *Mistress* or *Madame* when I was in charge. Apparently, Zed felt the same.

"I want to hear my *real* name on your tongue when I make you scream. Say nothing but my name. Get on all fours."

I tried to be as sexy as possible when I crawled over. I knew my ass was in his face. I knew he was supposed to be in charge and normally, I had no problem playing the role of a submissive, but I had Zed riled up. I wriggled my ass at him and was rewarded with a smack on the ass. It stung like hell and turned me on even more.

Zed wanted to give orders, so I just waited. He crawled over by the headboard and wanted me to wrap my hands around the carved wood post. He used my belt to tie my hands together, then crawled behind me and just seemed to do nothing. I knew he might spank me again, but I needed to know what the hell he was up to.

"Just admiring the view from behind," he growled. "It's hard not just to fuck you now that I have you like this, but it may ruin things for the apocalypse. We still don't know how that works."

"You promised me tricks. Would you finally touch me if I promised you there's something on the Taco Bell menu that's probably so bad for you, you'd come just eating it?"

He rewarded me with a smack on the ass again. "Don't rush me, Tabby. This is an art. The other three won't just feel this; they are going to hear you screaming my name."

"I didn't take you for a tease either."

Zed just chuckled. "Much like you are many things at once and quite the intriguing little thing, I have several tricks and want what I'm in the mood for. And right now, I'm in the mood for staring at that perky ass while you're tied up."

I felt Zed's erection press against my ass through the leather. Like Gideon, it was promising. He said I couldn't touch him, but he seemed content to just grind against me for the time being. Zed was much bigger than I was. He leaned forward so that he was on all fours too and his body was covering mine. He was supporting his weight with one hand, and the other went underneath me to pinch my nipple. He was biting my shoulder. Oh, I liked this. I wouldn't mind this position with his cock buried inside me.

He continued to bite my neck and pinch my nipple until I was whimpering and squirming. I felt his chest rumble as he chuckled. "So, I guess I did make you whimper."

His hand trailed down my stomach to rest on my clit. I groaned when his fingers barely brushed it. His entire body was hovering over me, but he wasn't crushing me. Zed was huge and could easily rest on all fours over me with my head down by the pillow and my ass in the air. I loved his warmth and closeness. And I loved the promise of that huge cock pressing against me.

I nearly screamed when he pulled away. He wanted me only to scream his name and I did when I felt his body leave mine. His fingers had only barely touched my clit, and I believe he promised me tricks tonight. That wasn't the kind of tricks I liked. And Zed was *laughing* at me. I felt his hand caress my ass.

"Easy, little lamb. Don't let the lion out. I just can't get to everything I want from that position."

Zed didn't make me wait. His hand slid between my legs and found my clit. He slid two fingers in me with the other hand and found something I was sure didn't exist because, despite a lot of men swearing they knew where it was, no one had found my G spot. I had no idea where it was or what it felt like before, but I knew Zed had found it almost immediately when my knees started shaking and I realized I'd never quite been fingered like this before.

The Horseman of Justice wasn't lying about tricks and skills. He was rubbing my clit with one hand and giving my g spot a workover with his other. I just about jumped out of my skin when I felt his tongue dip in my ass. Zed certainly wasn't lying about his tricks and skills. My entire body was shaking. Even if he hadn't told me I was only allowed to scream his name, I seemed incapable of doing anything but whimper and moan it.

Most guys I'd been with seemed just to want to make me come as fast as possible when they were doing anything with their fingers or mouth. Zed had this down to an art. He was just fast enough to have my entire body on fire and shaking, but he was keeping me at a state of constant pleasure instead of making me come just yet. His tongue was fucking my ass, and I was coming undone.

Now that I knew I actually had a g spot, I wanted Zed to play with it every night. Preferably with the other three Horsemen playing too. Yeah, even with Zed giving me the finger fuck of my life, I still thought about the others. That probably wasn't normal, but I didn't care.

It was almost too little to notice, but I could tell when Zed did decide to speed up. He was like a one-man orchestra, and I was his instruments. Zed was like the maestro of fingering, and if my body was shaking and on fire this much just from his fingers, I was already fantasizing about that bulge I felt and what would happen if I actually got his pants off.

I heard Zed chuckle again. "You're not screaming my name loud enough, little lamb. Let's fix that."

I wasn't screaming his name because I didn't think I was capable of anything more coherent than grunts and whispers, but Zed had to be magic. When he doubled his efforts, I started shrieking his name, and my orgasm was barreling at me at an alarming rate. When it hit me, I saw stars, and my body turned to Jell-O. I kept waiting for Zed to untie me. I was never a huge snuggler. I kicked people out of my apartment or left right after we were done. But I liked snuggling with Gideon, and I wanted to snuggle with Zed. That was certainly new for me, but so was everything else that had been thrown at me since Mattan showed up at my door.

I just laid there in this huge tied up heap on the bed. My body was still shaking, and Zed hadn't made a move to untie me yet.

"Um, Zed?" I said, trying to crane my head behind me.

Zed started laughing again. "Oh, that's cute, Tabby. You think that was the extent of my skills? I'm not even close to done with you tonight."

CHAPTER 20

Zed certainly had skills. He kept me awake screaming for hours and he never even took his pants off. He kept me tied to the bed and did all that with just his fingers. When he finally untied me and spooned himself into my back, he kissed the back of my head and swore he had other skills with his tongue and when he got his pants off. Zed was all on board with what I wanted and promised to talk to the others.

When I got to breakfast, I kept expecting everyone to be angry if they could feel me with the others. It wasn't like that with Gideon, and it wasn't like that when I walked to breakfast with Zed. It was weird. If they all had this history of dying because of a woman, why weren't they angry about it? They didn't even give me or Zed dirty looks when we got to breakfast a little late.

In fact, Chase grabbed me and pulled me into his lap. He slid my plate over to him like he intended to either feed me or have me eat there. That was when I saw the first dirty look between the four of them. Gideon was scowling at Chase.

"Chase, we need to tell her before you go all Horseman of Conquest because you don't want to wait for your night guarding her."

"Tell me what?" I asked, sliding the plate closer.

I had no idea I'd be into this until Jana brought it out to me, but Lox and bagels were getting right up there with waffles as one of my top breakfast foods. The Horsemen liked it too, so Jana had been serving it often. Of course, we all liked it slightly different. When this was served, Jana brought out like six different flavors of cream cheese and different flavored bagels. Some of us liked capers with ours. It was Jana that convinced me to put those little green brain looking thingies on my bagel, and now I wouldn't eat it any other way. I had no idea what a fucking caper was in the first place, but it was delicious on an everything bagel with jalapeno cream cheese.

I'd already inhaled half my bagel when I realized no one else was eating and they were all staring at me. I was pretty sure they were all used to me eating like a pig, and it wasn't because I was shoving the bagel in my face hole and making little happy noises.

"What?" I asked with a mouthful of food.

"Something strange. We don't know what it means yet," Gideon said, frowning at me.

"You can be a fucking moron sometimes, Gideon. Everyone knows what it means but you," Bash said.

I swallowed the bagel and Lox down and glared at all of them. "Someone care to clue me in because I don't know either."

"Well, you know we can feel each other, right?" Bash said, giving me this huge grin. "Last night, we felt *you* and we all ending up taking cold showers then jerking off because you just kept going. I can't speak for the others, but I wanted to kick your bedroom door in and fuck your brains out."

"We *all* did," Chase said, brushing my hair off my shoulders. "Gideon is coming up with conspiracy theories because he doesn't want to believe what you mentioned over breakfast the other day could be our solution to living out a long life on Earth *and* having a relationship."

"You're all just horny and thinking with your dicks. We showed up when the seals broke and saw Tabitha and a cat. What if Tabitha was the Antichrist this entire time and she's been tricking us?"

"I wasn't joking about sticking my boot up your ass when we first met," I growled. Had he totally forgotten that night in my bedroom when he was guarding me?

"Tabitha, please," Gideon sighed. "I'm just throwing out theories. None of us tried to date until after the Lamb was married. We stayed through the entire wedding. Sometimes, it was a century where there was a bedding ceremony. We *never* felt a Lamb get sexually aroused before. Nothing like last night."

"It started with Gideon," Chase said. "We could feel it just a little, but we didn't know what it meant. It became pretty fucking obvious last night when you went for a marathon play session with Zed."

"We're not here to have marathon play sessions with the Lamb!" Gideon snapped.

"That certainly didn't stop you from kissing me," I snapped. I was butthurt he actually thought I was the Antichrist and had been lying to them this entire time.

"I know, Tabby," Gideon sighed, finally calling me by my nickname instead of my full name like I was in trouble with him. "All I'm saying is that this is strange. Maybe it means what you keep suggesting over breakfast is possible and we can all be some polyamorous family. Or maybe it means Drake is somehow fooling all of us and if we do what you're wanting before we stop him, we all die. That would leave you and the witnesses vulnerable. He technically needs us for the apocalypse to happen, but maybe he knows something we don't. Maybe he thinks we're useless if we only follow you and he's got his own plans."

"Then why the fuck didn't you just say that instead of accusing *me* of being like my brother?"

"Because he doesn't know what the fuck he's doing or feeling and he thinks if he pushes you away, he doesn't have to think about this," Bash said, clapping Gideon on the back.

Gideon looked at me like he was in pain. "He's right. We can't protect you and stop Drake if we are dead. If I have to push you away until the damned apocalypse is over, I will."

I just shrugged. I thought this was progress and I actually thought this was a good thing. Me and my Horsemen were clearly connected at a deeper level than just the apocalypse.

"Did you ever think we are connected this way because it's going to help us stop Drake?" I pointed out.

Gideon's green eyes came up to meet mine. He actually looked hopeful for once. "Explain, Tabby."

"Well, if you can feel me, you'll know when I'm in danger. I get the feeling all of you work together so well for what you do because of what you can feel. Don't you think we'll be able to stop Drake better if we're a team on a deeper level?"

Bash's eyes bore into mine. "I want you to try something, Tabby. Something no Lamb before you has been able to do with us. I want you to concentrate. Blot out every single sound in the room and tell me if you can hear what I'm thinking."

I squinted my eyes and tried to concentrate. I swear, I was about to pop some vein in my forehead I was listening so hard. Could you die from that? Some big, gross vein in your forehead bursting because you're trying to see if you could read thoughts? I was starting to get a headache I was trying so hard. It wasn't until I gave up and tried to breathe to get the pounding in my head to stop that I finally heard Bash.

I grinned at him and winked. "You know you're going to have to show me that now, right?" He was thinking dirty thoughts about what he wanted to do with that promise he made about his tongue.

Gideon got excited, but it wasn't what *I* wanted him to be excited about. He wasn't thinking about all the naughty things we could do now. He was thinking about what I *should* have been thinking about — the fucking apocalypse.

"You're connected to us, and you can hear us. But Drake is your twin, and no matter how different you are, you are connected to him too. Now that we know you have this gift; can you sense him?"

"Will he know?" I asked. I didn't quite think this was a good idea.

Bash looked a little insane when he grinned at me. "If he does, maybe he'll let something slip. If he knows there's a line of communication open, maybe he'll tell you things Mattan doesn't want you to know. He might feel some connection to you because you're twins."

This was totally new to me. I'd never imagined I'd be able to hear thoughts before. I had no idea if it just worked on my Horsemen or I was turning into some sort of badass superhero. I'd always wanted to be able to fly. Maybe that would happen too. I guess I wasn't thinking about the Horsemen being able to read my thoughts too because Bash snorted like Lizzie.

"You're crazy, Tabby. You know that? You're not going to start flying or being able to turn invisible like in the movies."

"Can you blame me for going there? The cat knocked four stone circles on the floor, four hot men appeared, and now that cat is a real boy who happens to be the Antichrist. And he's rallying Incels. Don't forget about the Incels."

"Concentrate, Tabby," Zed said gently. "If you can safely talk to Drake from a distance, we may be able to stop the Antichrist and bring down some Incels too."

"I don't even know what Drake looks like when he's not some mutant cat in a purple sweater and I don't know where Mattan lives."

Chase jumped up and practically dropped me on the floor. He had pretty shitty manners for someone who bragged about being Conquest.

"She's right. It helps if she has a mental picture and I've got plenty of videos of Drake on my laptop. Come and see."

"You just love that line from the scripture, don't you?" Bash teased. "You know Tabby hasn't even read it and you aren't impressing her."

"Guy, seriously. I need to see Drake so I can try this."

Chase thankfully didn't show me any videos of Drake entertaining escorts or apparently jerking off to the dirty videos he recorded without the women's permission. He showed me a still photo he took of Drake answering the door.

My twin looked nothing like me. He looked nothing like Mattan either. I wondered who the hell he took after because it wasn't either of his parents. I remembered the videos when we were toddlers. Drake had long, black hair. It looked like it must have grown and never been cut while his body was in a coma and he hadn't bothered getting it cut once he was back in it.

Drake looked like he spent a lot of time on grooming since he became a real boy again. It looked like he was one of those girls in historical novels that sat in front of the mirror and wouldn't go to bed until they had brushed their hair one hundred times so it would shine. He was also sporting more eyeliner than I did and that said a lot. Drake was pale and kind of sickly looking from never going out in the sun. It looked like he wanted to keep that look.

Drake looked like he was trying way too hard to out Goth me. He looked like he was trying too hard to be Goth in general. He looked like a little poseur Lizzie and I would have made fun of.

Bash apparently understood my thought process. "I've been watching the videos too. He's not even into the right music. Like, none of the music. He likes to fuck to Taylor Swift, and I don't think he knows what Deathrock or Dark Cabaret is. He's not even trying to find out either. I think he just likes playing dress up."

"Yes, Drake's a tool," Gideon said, rolling his eyes. "He's the Antichrist, and he's preaching to Incels. We could make fun of Drake all day, but we forget he's dangerous and we need to stop him."

Bash just scooped me up like I weighed nothing and carried me over to the sofa. He sat down with me in his lap and wrapped his arms around me. I had my fuck me boots on so that Zed couldn't rub my feet. I already knew what he was doing. I finally heard Bash's thought when I relaxed. I needed to be relaxed to hear Drake and sitting in Bash's lap was like an instant chill pill. I was totally putty when he started playing with my hair.

Gideon cleared his throat. "*Relax* her, Bash. This isn't sexual."

"It's not," I said with heavily lidded eyes. "Just because he's touching me doesn't mean it's sexual, you perv. This is working. It's hard because I've never met Drake as a human."

"You still would have gotten vibes off him as a cat. What did you feel when you were around him?" Gideon said, finally trying to be helpful.

"Like I didn't know if he was a cat or a demon. I didn't know if I could trust the things I thought he was trying to show me. I thought I was losing my mind listening to a cat."

"That wasn't just because he was a cat. You're going to feel that while he's human too. Are you sure you want to do this? You're just supposed to break the seals," Zed said.

"We're all connected — the five of us, Lizzie and Ariel. We all do this together. I might not have badass Horsemen powers or breathe fire like Lizzie and Ariel, but I do have a connection to Drake none of you have. I'm doing this. Now, shut up."

I relaxed and focused on what I remembered of Drake as the cat. That wasn't working, so I decided to focus the videos of us as children. I felt like I was traveling through a tunnel and was suddenly in a lush room. I realized I was looking through Drake's eyes. Thankfully, he wasn't having happy fun time to one of his dirty videos. He was on a furious Twitter rampage to his Incel followers.

"Tabby? I didn't think you would reach out. I didn't think you could."

Drake sounded...happy to see me and a little sad. I decided to work that to my advantage. *"How did it get like this, Drake?'*

"You were planning to kill me, Tabby. You didn't even wait to hear my side. You were just going to have a vet do it."

"I was scared, Drake. Why did you trick me into breaking the seals before telling me the truth? I would have found a way to let you out of the cat if you hadn't pulled the magical cat act and tricked me into releasing the Horsemen."

"That was Mattan's grand idea. He thought if you heard me talking to you in your head, you'd flip out and send me to a kill shelter. I kept wanting to tell you, and Mattan kept talking me out of it."

"How the hell were you talking to Mattan? Was he sneaking in and out this house like some creepy pervert? He didn't spy on Lizzie while she was naked, did he? Do you know what he did to our mother?"

"I talked to Mattan the same way we are talking. I don't think you realize everything about our father, Tabitha."

"I refuse to call him that. He's a rapist, and he's trying to end the world."

"You don't understand. He can't help it. You know he's related to the Lambs, right? He's traced his lineage. He's got Rothledge blood too, just diluted because the thirteen families have been mixing for so long. It was just enough to give him certain abilities like being able to talk back to me when I realized who he was the first time I saw him, but not enough to be well, either of us."

"That doesn't excuse any of his behavior, Drake. Why are you following him after what he did?"

"Why are you defending our mother after what she did to me? How do you know if she hadn't loved me and spoiled me when I grew up, I would react the same way you do about Mattan if I

ever found out? She just shoved me in a cat for twenty-four years and stuck you in the middle of nowhere."

I knew what Drake was doing. He was trying to play on my sympathies. He was trying to use what our mother did to both of us to get me working with him and Mattan to break those seals. I wasn't falling for it. My bullshit radar worked even if I was using telepathy. Holy shit, I was using telepathy to talk to my twin, who was the Antichrist. Things just got weird, and they had been weird since Mattan showed up at my door. I think it had just gotten to the point of weirdness I was starting to wonder if someone had drugged my drink and I was passed out in an alley somewhere.

"Drake, this is all new to me. I need to figure all of this out. I didn't even know I could talk to you like this until now. I need time to figure things out. I don't think I can face Mattan, but I don't even know you. Can we call a truce? Neither of us makes a move until we've gotten to know each other and figured this out."

"Tabitha, you aren't just the Lamb meant for breaking seals. You're my twin. We shared a womb. When this is over, you'll have a place by my side. But I see you need more time. I want you to trust me. I want us to be real twins. I'll keep our father away from you, and maybe we can chat like this again."

"Drake, don't let me down. I can't trust someone who lets me down."

I shook my head to clear it and looked back at the Four Horsemen. They were all looking at me in awe. I had no idea if they could peek in and heard all that or I'd have to repeat everything.

"Tell us what Drake said and we'll tell you about the new mystery about our Lamb," Zed said.

I spilled the entire conversation, and Drake's big reveal about Mattan. It creeped me out a little. I was waiting for this big mystery they knew about me. Whatever it was, they sensed it or saw it while I was talking to Mattan.

Gideon was biting his lower lip. "Do you know what this means—Mattan having Rothledge and Lamb blood and raping Levana?"

"I should learn to play the banjo?" I asked, realizing how totally gross my lineage was.

"Tabby," Gideon groaned. I was shocked when Mister reserved Horseman who pooped on all my ideas about a really hot fivesome and thought I was the Antichrist earlier this morning pulled me into his lap. "Think about it. If Mattan's Rothledge blood were anywhere in this century, your grandparents would have mentioned it to you. Mattan's Rothledge blood was probably way before the Rothledges even adopted that name. It did mark him as a potential Antichrist, but he didn't have enough Rothledge blood to fulfill anything. It did gift *you* with a little something extra."

"Are you saying I'm the Antichrist too?" I shrieked.

"No, Mattan had no idea what he was doing when he raped your mother. He had no idea she'd have twins. We think he intended to find a way back inside for a second child because you need a Lamb to break the seals and an Antichrist for the apocalypse. Something must have happened that he couldn't get back inside or he couldn't sense Drake. You sharing a womb with Drake made you more somehow. Sort of another weapon against him."

"Someone had better start explaining because I just spoke to the Antichrist from across town *in my head* and my father is also apparently a cousin and something else."

Gideon was stroking my hair trying to calm me, and this was so strange coming from him. It was like he remembered our night together and was okay with it. Or he was scared of me now and didn't want me blowing anything up with my mind or joining Drake.

"Your eyes glowed white when you went into a trance to talk to Drake, Tabby," Gideon said, still stroking my hair. "The only beings we know that can do that are angels and us. None of the Lambs before you could do that. It probably explains why we are all so drawn to you, and you keep making all those inappropriate suggestions."

"What does that even mean? And it's not inappropriate. It's kinky fun."

Chase just laughed. "It's like you're the supercharged Lamb. You're like one of us. You might actually be able to fly or go invisible. You have gifts, and we just need to figure out what they are."

"You keep talking about the previous Lambs. How many were there and when was the last time you were here?"

Chase had his shoulder massages, and Zed had his foot rubs. Gideon's hands in my hair were my new favorite thing with Gideon. I hoped he kept doing it while someone explained.

"Every child with enough Lamb blood has the potential to break the seals. They've only been broken by accident three times. The four of us haven't been on Earth for nine hundred years. Maybe it's more than you and Drake being twins. Maybe someone up above decided to give you a little boost since Mattan wasn't playing fair," Bash said.

"I know what Tabitha has been gifted with," Gideon said. "It's so obvious, we all should have realized it once her eyes glowed. Tabitha is not just the Lamb. Lizzie and Ariel have the fire that will injure Drake and distract him. The breath of God is what blows him into the Lake of Fire. I'm almost one hundred percent certain it's been bestowed on Tabitha to stop Drake. All of us, we're meant to stop this before it goes too far."

"You're telling me my superpower is to burp on Drake and he goes to hell?" I asked. "Well, that's not as fun as flying."

I heard Gideon chuckle, and his arms went around my waist to pull me to his chest. He kissed the top of my head. I was starting to think something was wrong with Gideon. He was never like this.

"Well, we can show you fun. If you aren't any regular human woman, then maybe those ideas you keep getting about all of us are what's supposed to happen. You might not be able to fly, but once we stop Drake, we can make some of those fantasies of yours come true. Not until after we've stopped the apocalypse just in case I'm wrong, but I'd like to explore our little tryst on the sofa a little further."

After everything I'd heard today, and since I got here, those words from Gideon had to be the craziest thing today.

Chapter 21

The Four Horsemen of the Apocalypse has to be the biggest vagina teases I'd ever met. No, we can't fuck you, sure, we'll all fuck you, but not until we stop the apocalypse and knock your evil twin back to hell. If this were a porn video, I would have stopped watching ages ago and picked something with a little more instant gratification. Most dudes I knew were pretty eager to fuck when you asked them, but not these four. Oh, no, I couldn't give my kinky fivesome until the damned apocalypse was over. Who said that anyway?

After they all but agreed to make all my kinky fantasies with them come to life, then told me I had to fucking wait, Lizzie and Ariel finally came over. Lizzie thought my new powers were awesome and it was about time I got some since she could breathe fire. My grandparents came over shortly after Lizzie and Ariel did, and I *had* to know if they knew about Mattan's Rothledge blood and how closely he was related to my mother.

My Oma and Opa exchanged looks. "The Adlers and the Rothledges have never married into each other, but there's a story that goes back to just before the Salem Witch Trials. A Rothledge cousin on the side of the family the other Rothledges had a falling out with fell in love with an Adler son. A younger son who wouldn't inherit anything. There were rumors they ran away and married.

"The Adler's used to have trouble conceiving. Every generation struggled to produce an heir up until recent inventions with modern fertility treatments. It used to be this dirty little Adler secret everyone knew about. If it got to the point it looked like the Adler's weren't going to have an heir, they would take anyone with Adler blood if they could prove it. It used to be done by heirlooms because DNA tests weren't a thing back then. It's entirely possible the child of the Rothledge cousin and the Adler son came back to Salem and was claimed as an Adler heir. The Rothledge *and* Adler blood would have been diluted at that point, but that wouldn't have mattered to the Adlers. They just wanted a little Adler blood to carry on the line," Opa said.

"How did the Adlers get Lamb blood?" I asked, trying to figure out my exact lineage.

"Well, the Rothledge connection was over four hundred years ago from what I understand," Sabba said. "The Lambs and the Adlers go back sixty years. The Lamb family is rather large. Elliot had two brothers and three sisters, and you have several nieces, nephews, and cousins running around. It was a huge scandal at the time. The second daughter of a Lamb cousin either fell for or was seduced by an older, widowed Adler. He would have been the Adler patriarch at the time, and his wife had only been gone a month when he started spending time with the seventeen-year-old Lamb girl.

"Her parents refused to give permission, but they eloped. She would have been Mattan's mother. Mattan would have been a third or fourth cousin to Elliot, but he does have a strong connection to the Lambs. He's always preferred the company of Adlers and as far as everyone knew, was never close with his mother."

Okay, so over four hundred years ago. Maybe I didn't need to start banjo lessons and actually watch the movie *Deliverance*. It was a long time ago. I felt a little better. I was hoping to keep my new superpowers a secret from my grandparents. I didn't want them to worry because if I was the one who had the power to blow Drake straight to hell, I was going to have to get close.

Gideon had a big fucking mouth. He spilled everything. Mattan's big secret, my glowing eyes, and that he thought Heaven had gifted me. He slung his arm around my shoulder like he thought I was one of the boys and dubbed me the fifth

Horseman. It sounded a lot like he just dumped me in some Horseman buddy club friend zone.

Clearly, Oma saw something I was missing. She was giving all four Horsemen epic grandmother stink eye. Her eye landed on me, and I shifted uncomfortably.

"If they get fresh with you, you smack them and remind them why they are here."

Oh, Oma, I wanted them to get fresh with me. I wanted them to get ass naked and kinky with me. Lizzie pinched my arm because I must have been in the kinky fun zone instead of paying attention.

"Does any of that help us stop them?" Lizzie asked, saving my ass again.

"Well, we'd know if Drake was honoring the truce if The Four Horsemen were watching the computer again instead of staring at my granddaughter that way!" my Oma snapped.

Chase was the furthest away from me and hopped up to get his laptop. "He's got to be pretty stupid if he thinks we haven't found his accounts yet."

"Maybe not," I pointed out. "They probably had no idea the Horsemen know computers this go around and Mattan probably thinks Lizzie and I are too poor to have computers. We still have phones, and we both completed high school."

"We probably knew about Twitter before that shit head did because we weren't stuck in a cat," Lizzie snapped.

Lizzie was practically glowing, and Natalia wasn't there. I wondered what was up and I needed alone time with Lizzie. I knew I wasn't going to get it quite yet. Ariel proved handy to have around yet again.

"What about the Mark of the Beast? Isn't Drake supposed to have it? Would Mattan have a faint one? Does anyone know what the Mark is?"

Bash just snorted. Lizzie's signature snort was getting contagious. "I wouldn't put it past that little wanker to be tattooing 666 on his forehead because he thinks it makes him more goth. The Mark of the Beast isn't a birthmark or something that would announce Drake or Mattan as the Beast. Drake is going to be looking for someone, a false prophet to build up his followers. The false prophet will have his followers put the Mark of the Beast on them to signify they follow Drake. The Mark is supposed to be his name, but Drake may go in a different direction."

Now it was my turn to catch the snorting. I was starting to wonder if the whole room was getting hexed to be put into hogs like Drake was put into that cat.

"Doesn't *anyone* know the name rule? I'm sure it works with the fucking Antichrist too. Pretty much as soon as you become psycho enough to tattoo someone's name on your ass or worse, your forehead, they are going to feel the stalker vibes and run," I said. How did no one know this? Even if you didn't have any ink on your skin, it had to be common knowledge that putting someone's name on your skin permanently with divorce rates and commitment-phobes today was going to be stupid.

"I don't think Drake decided to go for Incels just because he was pissed about not getting laid because he was stuck in a cat," Chase said. "I understand it because I'm the Horseman of Conquest. Drake needs an army of *angry* followers who subscribe to an ideal he can twist. A misguided, horrible idea he can use to his advantage. If Drake and his chosen prophet get them on his side, they will think it's an honor to tattoo the mark. As the number of people with Drake's mark grows, the more it will inflame his ego. Your name rule doesn't work with the Antichrist."

Well, fuck. It still counted a little, and we had a plan. We would ruin Drake's little Incel army before they even had a chance to tattoo his fucking name on their asses. We had videos and all his social media sites. We were missing something very important though.

"Who is the false prophet?" I asked. "If we out Drake, he'll still have the false prophet behind him."

"Drake isn't stupid, even if he's been stuck in a cat for twenty-four years," Gideon said. "Drake is going to network. He's not just going to recruit the Incels. I will bet money Mattan has a role as a prophet in some sort a business sector *and* he's giving Drake and his follower's legal advice to not get caught."

My shoulders slumped. The apocalypse was so fucking complicated. Every time I thought we had a plan, Drake had more trickery and plots. Oma scowled at Gideon when he started playing with my hair then she scowled at me when I turned into an instant wad of putty.

"You forget, we're watching Drake and Mattan. We can see all Drake's private messages. He hasn't been human long," Bash said. "You can't just post an ad on a job site for a false prophet. Use your head before becoming totally hopeless, Tabby. Drake and Mattan have to convince people to follow Drake, and with all the cynicism in the world today, that is going to take time. No one is going to believe either of them if he says he's the Antichrist. The Church of Satan doesn't even believe in Satan and would think he was full of shit if he approached them claiming to be the Antichrist."

I realized I was just freaking out for nothing. Well, not totally nothing. My twin was the Antichrist, and I now had superpowers. But the apocalypse wasn't going to happen overnight just because I released the Horsemen. I didn't even have three thousand twitter followers, and I'd had an account for ages. Lizzie had some sort of cult following on Instagram because she posted photos of all the outfits she made. She really could have made more money sewing than she did bartending, but both of us were too neurotic about money to quit our job and dive into the unknown. Even Lizzie didn't have the followers Drake would need.

We still needed to move quickly, but we had time.

Chapter 22

My grandparents all had to leave for business meetings, but they wouldn't leave until they were content I didn't have any questions they could answer, the Four Horsemen swore to my Oma they were going to behave, and we all watched Mattan and Drake. They promised to come back in the morning to see if they could answer anything I might not know and they wanted to spend time with me.

Drake spent most of the day on the computer. There were several men he was talking to, but he appeared to want to know details for one particular man. He was looking for a man named Hannibal Bates Even if Lizzie hadn't told me he was sort of a god to the Incels, his name creeped me out. With a name like that, he was probably a budding serial killer who snuck into women's houses and stole their panties. He probably had a collection of toenails and liked to talk about how he wondered what human flesh tasted like over family dinners. I was guessing he still lived in his parent's basement in a room surrounded by fast food wrappers.

Drake wanted Hannibal as his prophet, but it didn't appear like Hannibal wanted to give him the time of day. We watched Mattan too. He wasn't doing anything sinister, but he was moving money around to different stocks and posting on stock forums. Chase seemed to know the most about what Mattan was up to. Mattan was trying to find a way to manipulate the stock market and the people who invested.

We watched until they both took a break for their nightly escort visits. The Horsemen understood me and Lizzie's connection and shooed us away to just record what we needed. Lizzie had been antsy and glowing at the same time all day. We needed to talk. Natalia was gone all day, and I wondered if they had fought. I tried to pull Lizzie to my bedroom, but she told me she would be right back.

She came back with a million garment bags. Did Lizzie have time to sew in the middle of the apocalypse?

"Lizzie, what's going on? What's with all the clothes and why wasn't Natalia with us today?"

Lizzie practically shrieked. "She's planning our first date. A date instead of sneaking into someone's apartment. She said she was making reservations, so it's probably got classy food and shit instead of the places we normally eat at. Odelia was trying to help me figure out which fork to use. I still don't understand why there's more than one. A fork is for putting food in your face. Why does there need to be a different one for the salad than there is for the main food? It's ridiculous! They all work the same, and you still get full even if you grab the wrong fork."

I grabbed Lizzie into a headlock hug and just laughed. "Fuck the forks. You've got a hot date with someone who cares enough to take you out for once. How do Esther and Odelia feel about the two of you dating?"

Lizzie moaned. "They are practically planning the wedding. How are things with your hot Horsemen?"

"Lord, girl, Zed would give you a run for your money with your claim you can finger a girl better than anyone on the planet."

"Ha!" Lizzie snorted. "That's because I'd never finger you, you wench. Have you decided on Zed or are you still being a greedy bitch and want all of them?"

I explained to Lizzie what would happen if I chose just one and that I probably wanted all four of them for a reason. She just nodded like she understood.

"Why am I not surprised magic vagina is the only thing that can kill a Horseman?"

"Lizzie!" I shrieked, shoving her arm. "I think there's more to it than that. It's something about a broken heart, not a supernatural STD."

"So, Gideon got you off with all your clothes on, and Zed has magic fingers. Who is guarding you tonight? Maybe Zed and I can talk about the trade secrets of fingering."

"Bash is guarding me tonight, and he swears he's got oral skills."

"If you start telling me they are better than mine tomorrow, I'm going to swear you're just being mean."

"Hey, you've got gorgeous Natalia to impress, not me. I've seen you in the morning with your hair everywhere and your face melting off because you went to bed with your makeup on again."

"I'm going to need some help with the runt," Lizzie said, leaning back on my bed. "I swear, she's like my Mini-Me. She wants to find Drake's Incel followers and blow fire on them. She's pissed, and she's going to get careless."

"We'll all help with Ariel. Now, I believe you have a date to go get ready for."

CHAPTER 23

I spent so much time with Lizzie trying to pick the perfect custom dress for her date, by the time we had decided, she was rushing out the door, and the Horsemen had all taken up guard duty. Bash was guarding me tonight, and I believe he threw a gauntlet about his oral skills. I grinned and headed up to my room. Maybe now that they all agreed I was connected to them, I could also get laid tonight.

My jaw dropped when I threw open my bedroom door. Bash was sprawled out on my bed in a very tiny, black leather G-string. He was pale as fuck, but I guess that was because he was Death. Death looked really hot in a thong. I went sprinting towards my bed and practically tackled him. This was cause for celebration.

"Finally, I get one of you to take your pants off," I growled, going to pull that G-string off.

Bash caught my hands and clucked his tongue at me. "You're still not getting dick from any of us until the apocalypse is over. We still don't know what will happen."

"Then why are you in that thong?" I wailed. The Horsemen were such muffin muzzles. I wanted dick, damn it.

Bash gave me this evil grin and pinned me on my back. He held my hands over my head with one of his and licked the tip of my nose. I normally would have found that disgusting, but I guess Death in a thong could make it sexy.

"Payback, Tabby. Don't think I haven't noticed your corsets getting lower and your skirts getting shorter since you decided you didn't want to put those sexy boots up our asses."

"Well, clearly, you all have balls of steel because *none* of you will get naked with me. And now you're torturing me," I pouted.

"Oh, honey," Bash chuckled. "You've got the Horseman of Death in bed with you. I'm going to show you exactly why they used to call the orgasm *la petite mort.* You won't be pouting when I'm done with you."

Bash didn't even give me the chance to give any type of witty retort back. He crushed his lips to mine, and I parted my lips when I felt his tongue wanting to enter. I got a little light headed. Bash kissed totally different than Gideon or Zed. With Gideon, there was this explosion of passion he always held back. Zed took his time when he was kissing you, like he had all the time in the world to pleasure you. With Bash, it was like this all-consuming kiss where he took a part of my soul with him. I was panting when he broke the kiss.

I couldn't move at all. Bash had my hands pinned over my head and most of his body weight on me. I wondered if he was going to tie me up like Zed did. I was all for being tied up and tongue fucked if that's where Bash was headed. His eyes roamed down to my cleavage. Maybe I had been going overboard with my corset choices lately. I normally didn't wear them around the house and every day, but I was trying to snag four Horsemen with a death vagina that could kill all four of them.

Bash kissed the tip of my nose and climbed off me. My eyes immediately went to the front of that leather G-string. He was lucky he moved away from me because the outline of his cock was so promising I was about to rip the damn thing off with my bare hands. I had no idea what the fuck he was doing when he left my bed and went and sat in an overstuffed chair. He had a remote ready and queued music.

He leaned back and started stroking that huge bulge under the thong. His eyes were hooded as he stared at me. Maybe I would get him naked.

"You spend so much time getting in that corset and those boots in the morning. I want to watch you get *out* of them."

I cocked an eyebrow at him. "You want a striptease? What do I get? You already said you aren't taking that thong off."

"I felt you last night, remember? I spent forty-five minutes trying to take a cold shower and ended up jerking off three times before you were finished playing with Zed. You know full well all four of us have skills to please you without taking our pants off just yet. Be patient, my lion."

Bash would get his striptease, but I was doing it my way. Bash tried to make a point about my clothing by teasing me with his little thong. Maybe he didn't know I worked at a strip club and after dragging tips out of horny men, I wrote the fucking book on teasing. Bash was getting his striptease with a little side of Tabitha revenge. Maybe I'd even get that thong off him.

Bash picked my favorite music to do a striptease to. He had a playlist of Dark Cabaret, and I knew every song. My skirt was tiny. I danced over to Bash and put one of my fuck me boots right at the side of his face.

"Unbuckle my boot with your teeth," I ordered. Zed may have tied me down the night before, but trust me, I'd fully explored my dominant side in addition to my submissive. I liked what I was in the mood for that night, and I was in the mood to fuck with the Horseman of Death tonight.

I didn't take Bash for being submissive at all. I wanted to rile him up. I was shocked when huge, bald Bash who looked like he crushed skulls outside one of the goth clubs I visited groaned and went to work on my buckles with his teeth. Was the Horseman of Death my puppy tonight?

Apparently not. Bash undid the buckles on one boot, yanked it off, then forgot all about that striptease he wanted. He growled and picked me up, carrying me over to the bed. He was the one that took my other boot off and unlaced my corset. He was grumbling about laces and buckles the entire time.

"I love seeing you in this getup, but it's a pain in the ass getting you *out* of it. Next time we do this, can you wear something without so many laces?"

"Next time we do this, can you be totally naked?"

Bash peeled my corset back and buried his face in my breasts. "I want to be naked with you as much as you want to be naked with me. It's hard waiting for us just like it is for you. We just have thousands of years of history to think about before we do anything about it. We all are ninety-nine percent sure being with you is not going to kill us, but it's the one percent we need to worry about until Drake is taken care of. You could help by not bringing it up all the time. We want it too; we just have to wait."

"I know," I groaned as Bash planted kisses all over my breasts. "I know why we have to wait. I know my vagina could be poison for all of you. I know I should be focusing on the apocalypse. It's just when I'm around all four of you, it just feels like that's what we're supposed to be doing."

Bash started focusing his attention on my neck, giving me little love bites. "I can't tell if you're just a horny little minx or you're onto something. I don't want to talk anymore, Tabby. I've been thinking about this for days. All I've wanted is to make you scream."

Bash was a biter, and I loved every minute of it. I wanted him to kiss me again. Bash hadn't even used those special oral skills he bragged about, and I was begging for his kisses. All the Horsemen had kissing skills better than anyone I'd been with before, but I craved Bash's kisses right now. I wasn't thinking about kinky fivesomes. I was solely focused on the pale, muscular man in my bed who took my breath away when he kissed me.

Bash indulged me and kissed me for as long as I wanted. He finally pulled away and gave me this evil grin. "I promised to kiss you in other places too. Can I make you scream or do you want me to keep kissing you? Your wish is my command."

I wasn't feeling dominant and wanting to torture Bash anymore. I wanted a little more of Bash's brand of torture.

"Fuck, Bash. You bragged of skills. Show me everything. Surprise me."

Bash chuckled and started kissing his way down my belly button. "Never ask the Horseman of Death to surprise you, even in bed. Hold on tight, little lamb. You're in for a hell of a ride."

Bash didn't even give me time to react. He yanked my ass up and threw my legs over his shoulders. He set me back down gently, but seemed to want my thighs wrapped around his head. He even gave me a love bite with his face buried in my pussy. His little bites were driving me crazy. They were just hard enough to hurt a little and mix pleasure with pain, just the way I liked it.

I loved Bash's bald look, and he pulled it off quite sexily, but I was starting to wish he had some hair to pull. I was squirming as he fucked me with his tongue. He hadn't even gone for my clit yet, and I was already coming undone. His tongue slipped out of me and trailed up to my clit.

Like Zed, Bash knew how to take his time. He wasn't just trying to get this over with. Bash drew wave over wave of pleasure from me with every swirl of his tongue. Bash knew where the mysterious G spot was too. Two fingers slid inside my pussy and started massaging it in addition to his tongue. I was begging, pleading, screaming Bash's name. He was just eating me out like he had all night. And I had a feeling he just might do that.

I nearly screamed for him to go back when Bash stopped massaging that G spot I just found out I had. I wanted his fingers back when they left. I realized Bash had more tricks up his sleeve. Bash's fingers slid back in, but his other two fingers easily slid into my ass. His tongue finally sped up, and he started fucking me hard with his fingers.

After being teased for so long, my entire body was on fire. I was racing towards a massive orgasm and Bash showed no signs of slowing down. I was bucking and screaming his name. When my orgasm hit, I practically shrieked loud enough to wake the entire house. Bash didn't have any hair, so I just grabbed his ears and held on for dear life.

When I finally settled down, Bash kissed his way back up to my mouth and pulled me down to his chest. I snuggled in and tried for his thong again. A little blow job couldn't kill them, right? He just ate the shit out of me, and I wanted to return the favor. I wanted to return the favor with all of them, but only Bash took his pants off.

He caught my hand and just cracked up laughing. Bash was laughing so hard, the bed was shaking. I got the giggles too, but probably not for the same reason. Not many people could say they faced Death in a thong and lived to tell about it. No, I had Death in my bed, gotten clit fucked, and now he was laughing. Let my Antichrist twin brag about *that*.

"I don't know what you're laughing at," Bash wheezed. "You know, every time the seals broke, and we appeared before a Lamb, they were these little cherubs who thought *we* were angels. We appear this time to a purple haired badass threatening to put some sexy boots up our asses. Then, you totally turned it around and started wanting some sort of group thing with us. There's not much that can surprise the Four Horsemen of the Apocalypse, but you're like this little fun bag of wonders. What changed your mind about us? We haven't shown you any of our powers."

"Well, what was I supposed to think when the cat started speaking to me in my head? You didn't need to show me some Horseman powers. It was weird. After hearing Drake and all the chaos that followed, I just felt like I could trust you. You're all fun to be around too. After everything that's happened, Lizzie and I found each other like we were supposed to and finding out we're all supposed to stop the apocalypse is not the dumbest thing that has happened to me."

Bash kissed the top of my head and pulled me to his chest. "And how trusting us turned into you wanting to play house in some polyamorous relationship with the Four Horsemen?"

I just shrugged. That was pretty bizarre for me too. Normally, even one guy got on my nerves, and I was planning exit strategies after the second date. It just felt like this was what was *supposed* to happen. I was never one of those teenagers drawing my name in hearts with a dude's name. I never saw wedding bells with anyone. I wasn't seeing wedding bells now. But I could see myself waking up in that huge bed with the Four Horsemen and doing things that didn't involve stopping Drake. Maybe one of them could teach me to drive.

Bash seemed to understand my shrug. His finger traced the tattoos on my arm. He decided to tease me. "You always talk about being broke. How'd you afford the ink? This isn't flash done by a scratcher."

"There are two answers for that. When I moved in with Lizzie, she was dating this cute little tattoo artist. Honestly, she was the only one of Lizzie's girlfriends I ever liked. She'd tattoo both of us while watching Netflix to build work for her portfolio. She went to a tattoo convention, got drunk, and cheated on Lizzie.

That was the last I saw of her. The rest of my tattoos are what we broke folk call Tax Return Tattoos."

"Why didn't you use your tax return for food, you crazy girl?"

"Tax Return Tattoos take careful planning. It's like getting free money, so you don't want to spend it on something boring like rent. In the months leading up to your refund, you start picking up extra shifts and working overtime. That way, you've got it planned in case there are any surprises when you get your return. So, when your return comes in, if everything goes to plan, you've got tattoo money *and* extra money for food and rent."

Bash squeezed me so hard I couldn't breathe. It was actually nice. I felt safe with Bash, even if he was squeezing all the damned air out my lungs.

"I'm glad you don't have to worry about that anymore. None of us will let Drake hurt you, Lizzie, or Ariel. I can feel the same things you do, Tabby. It's not a coincidence that you could hear us when we asked. You're connected to us at a deeper level than any Lamb we've encountered when we've been released before. I'm starting to wonder if we just need to give you what you want and get naked with you because it's going to activate some gift we don't know about."

"You didn't know I was supposed to go all Breath of God and blow Drake straight to hell?"

"That actually shocked the hell out of all of us. You're just supposed to break the seals, not stop the Antichrist."

"I have a question," I said. This had been bothering me since I found out the truth about my parentage and history. "If someone was watching and knew Mattan was forcing the apocalypse, why didn't anyone just kill Drake and me when we were babies?"

"Oh, Tabby. Our side doesn't kill babies. The choices were always yours. Drake would always be the Antichrist, but he would be powerless without you to break the seals. Drake can start building armies and false prophets, but he can't actually do anything unless you finish starting the apocalypse."

"He's plotting something to get me to break those seals. He's not just making up for being a cat for so long by fucking escorts and preaching to Incels. Drake will have a plan."

"Drake doesn't know you have the power to send him to the fires of Hell. None of us knew. Drake can try, but he's going to see the Horsemen's power close up, Lizzie and Ariel will torture him with fire, then he'll see what the Lake of Fire is like up close. Whatever Drake's plan is to get to you, he won't succeed."

That made me feel a little better, but we were dealing with the Antichrist here and his fucked-up Daddy Mattan. If I had powers, Drake probably did too. He didn't know about mine. No one did. Tomorrow, I needed to find out what the Horsemen knew about Drake's powers.

CHAPTER 24

Hand holding and public displays of affection used to gross me out. I used to think if someone was trying that hard to show off in public that they were in love, there was probably some sort of problem they didn't want people to know about. So, don't ask me why I walked to breakfast holding hands with three Horsemen now. And it felt damned good too. Maybe I was just being mean with the people out in public before. I did have a habit of being a crabby bastard most of the time.

Chase was scowling when I sat down. "You know you made Conquest wait, right? Three nights now."

I grinned at Chase. He was so proud of being Conquest, and he'd already bragged about me being one of his. I decided to poke Chase a little because he was pouting.

"*I* didn't make you wait. All of you decided on the guarding order. If you were *really* Conquest, you would have demanded to guard me first or had the schedule changed."

Gideon snorted. "She's right, you know. You haven't been playing dirty this go. Are you sure you're feeling okay?"

Chase finally stopped pouting and looked serious for a minute. "Because I can feel this is different. I can feel Tabby likes all of us for different reasons and I don't think she has any intention of picking one of us. I'm fine with that, but did you ever think if I got up to my old tricks, whatever is supposed to happen won't work because I've driven Tabby away? My tricks won't work on her. She'd just punch me or do what she threatened and stick that fuck me boot up my ass. It has to be *all* of us. If I'm excluded, then we all just die again."

Everyone was nodding like that made sense. Gideon's intense eyes rest on me. "Can you sense what is supposed to happen if we get together? Do we all get extra powers and you get stronger?"

"I've got no idea. It just feels like it's supposed to happen on its own time though. I know I keep begging for it, but it needs to happen when everyone is on board, and there's no doubt. I don't think there's a rush. We do need to figure out what Drake is doing."

"True," Chase said. He was giving me that grin again like he was the Horseman of Conquest. "Care to sit in my lap while I look at computer stuff?"

I hadn't been with Chase at all yet. I wanted to sit in his lap and just answered with a wink. I was a little surprised when we got to the living room that Odelia, Esther, Lizzie, and Ariel were all there with computers. Natalia was there snuggled into the sofa with Lizzie. Clearly, date night went well. I was going to have to pick her brain later.

Chase grabbed my waist and crashed into the sofa with me. I had no idea how he intended to manage me and the laptop until he set the computer in my lap. He seemed more content to nuzzle my neck than look at the laptop. Good thing Gideon was also good on computers. Ariel had her laptop out and hadn't said a word.

"This is interesting," Gideon said. "Drake and Mattan both have very specific tastes with the escorts. Mattan has been trying to get a Gothic Lolita for Drake since he started getting escorts. Mattan gets the same type of woman every time. He likes submissive, eighteen-year-old blondes. They are both chatting with new women outside the escort site."

It had to be a toss-up between who was dry heaving the most out of Lizzie and me. Why was my family so creepy? Drake *and* Mattan had creeped on Lizzie and probably Ariel. I was wrapped up in making gagging noises. When Odelia shrieked, Lizzie screamed too and flung her coffee cup across the room. I nearly leapt off Chase's lap.

"Ariel Belcourt!" Odelia yelled. She looked *pissed*. "If that's you, I swear to all that's holy, I'm taking away your laptop. I've already grounded you once for extorting perverts. Is the mystery woman asking for money?"

Ariel looked totally calm and wasn't talking. Gideon was looking anywhere except Odelia. I was trying not to laugh. Was the little runt blackmailing my pervert of a twin and father? Lizzie pulled herself out of Natalia's lap and went and slung an arm around Ariel's shoulder.

"I think she's a genius if she is. She's probably getting intel and getting money to buy clothes at the same time."

"I am!" Ariel insisted. "I've been researching the Book of Revelations. There's something none of you have considered. Drake is *the* Beast, but there's more than one beast in the bible. I've got Mattan pegged as the Leopard-like Beast. The one who is supposed to be the new Babylon? Think about it. It makes sense. And if one of you Horsemen calls me a runt, I'm going to take your balls off. Only my sister is allowed to call me that!"

I was trying so hard not to laugh. Ariel was probably just under five feet tall and ninety pounds soaking wet. She looked *just* like Lizzie as she glared at the Horsemen threatening to take a testicle off. Odelia apparently wasn't done yet.

"You aren't doing this, Ariel. I've already grounded you once for this. You're too young to be talking to older men, and it's wrong to take their money. I don't want you talking to the Antichrist and whatever beast Mattan might be either! I don't want you doing it either, Lizzie! Let the Horsemen do it."

"Mom!" Ariel shrieked. "The Four Horsemen of the Apocalypse just *cannot* pretend to be girls and seduce the Antichrist. Drake has a Gothic Lolita fetish. Lizzie and I are perfect for doing this."

I could just tell there was about to be a screaming match. Lizzie looked ready to boot up and defend Ariel and Odelia looked like she was about to explode.

"Why don't we find out what Ariel has learned before we get upset with her?" I suggested. "It sounds like she's done a lot of research."

Lizzie shot me a grateful look. Natalia went over to sit next to Lizzie and hold her hand. Yeah, Natalia was right up there as my top favorite girlfriend for Lizzie. Ariel stood and did this epic hair flip. She started pacing the room.

"I didn't find out much from Mattan. I just needed to get into his computers to get his passwords. Drake wants a queen for when he's ruling heaven and earth beside Lucifer. Apparently, something clicked the first time he saw Lizzie, and he likes the way she smells. He wants Lizzie, but he'll take someone like her. I think he wants to kill Lizzie to rid her of witness powers and then when she's resurrected, he'll try to take her as his queen. Drake likes to talk a little more than Mattan so I think I can get more out of him."

Chase was absentmindedly rubbing the back of my neck. "What makes you think Mattan is the Leopard-like beast?"

"Because my research said the Leopard-like beast is going to be an empire like Babylon. The Adlers have a huge coffee empire, but Mattan became a lawyer. One of the things he bragged about when I was chatting with him was that he's putting his name forth for the next senate election. Claimed he could be my Dom because he would be a powerful politician. I don't think he quite understands the dominant/submissive relationship. I think he just likes hurting women and bossing them around. That's not how it goes at all."

"And you're seventeen and shouldn't know that!" Odelia snapped. "I swear, I'm going to lock you in your bedroom with no electronics or Wi-fi for the rest of your life."

Gideon went up a notch in my book when he defended the runt. Ariel had done a damned good job. I didn't want Lizzie's little sister talking to creepy pervs either, and that was probably why none of us knew about it, but she had done a *damned* good job for a seventeen-year-old.

"None of us want Ariel doing this," Gideon said, standing to place a protective hand on Ariel's shoulder. "Ariel may be seventeen, but you should be proud of her for being an intelligent, capable teenager instead of getting mad at her for knowing things you don't think she should know. Ariel successfully fooled *two* beasts. I think she's right about Mattan being the Leopard-like beast. This is all going so out of order."

"That's because Ariel is a little badass," Lizzie said. "So, Tabby burps on Drake and sends him to hell, how do we stop Mattan?"

"The two of you can burn him. He's *a* beast, not *the* Beast. Tabby will need to kill him the same way she does Drake. Drake and Mattan are playing the long game," Chase said. "They must think they have everything in hand with us if they can play long-term like this."

I leaned back into Chase's chest. If he kept making those circles on my neck, I was going to rip his pants off and fuck him in front of everyone. I needed to be thinking about Drake and Mattan, not sex right now.

"I think Drake wants me by his side," I said. "Drake wants a brother-sister relationship with me. He hasn't reached out to me because he wants me to come to him. He's going to use trickery to get me on his side, but I think he thinks that's love. One of you assholes had better tell me. If I'm getting superpowers, does Drake have any?"

"Deception," Zed said. "Drake has a silver tongue. He's going to be able to twist any event to his gain, and he can create chaos with just a few words. There have been theories that the Beast can use illusions to help with his deceptions, but opinions are divided."

"Well, someone better start sharing opinions and theories because we're all in danger," Lizzie snapped. "The runt isn't the only one who can take off your balls."

I was starting to really like Odelia. "My daughters aren't the only ones who can take off your balls. You've got a mama bear here with two daughters you've been telling me are supposed to die. I don't give a shit if you tell me they are supposed to be resurrected. If one of my children gets a scratch, all four of you are going to get a much bigger wound."

Lizzie needed that. She didn't think she did. She didn't think she needed anyone, but Lizzie needed some big, overprotective mother coming in showing her how much she loved her. I didn't want Lizzie to die either even if she got to come back, but I was glad she got to hear Odelia get that protective over her. I needed to hear my Horsemen be protective of her too or I was going to have to rescind my offer of a fivesome.

Gideon shocked me again. He got up and gave Odelia this huge hug, and it looked like he actually meant it. He towered over her by over a foot, but he looked like he was trying to soothe her. His eyes were looking directly at me, like he knew I had things I needed to hear too.

"Just because it's written Lizzie and Ariel die doesn't mean it will happen on our watch. If we can finally decide on a plan to stop Drake and Mattan, all this stops, and all of you can just live normal lives."

I gulped. I saw the look he was giving me. He said all of *you.* He said nothing about the Horsemen. Were they all keeping something from me? Trying to keep me happy while they were here by indulging my little bedroom fantasies, but once Drake was in the Lake of Fire, they were all just going to go poof?

I couldn't ask that right now. We needed a plan. We needed Drake and Mattan in front of us to send them to the Lake of Fire. Drake was the master of deception, but I think he didn't see clearly when it came to my lies. He wanted us to have a magical twin bond. Our plans for exposing Drake to the Incels would break some of Drake's trust in me, and I may not get my chance to face him before things got worse.

I needed Drake and Mattan in front of me with their guards down. They didn't know about my gifts. They didn't know we were in their computers. They didn't know their new online girlfriends were seventeen-year-old Ariel.

Maybe they wouldn't see us coming.

CHAPTER 25

The only normal part of my day now was after all the spying and plotting was that Lizzie and I would go to the secret room Odelia and Esther showed us the first day and just rant. We'd talk about our love lives and drink from my parent's pretty dope liquor stash. The chocolate truffles hidden in this room that Esther and Odelia showed us keep magically refreshing itself. I was almost certain it was Jana. At the rate she was going, all the employees here were going to be millionaires, and I was going to be dead ass broke again because I kept giving them raises.

We both crashed on the comfortable couch with our booze in hand and a box of truffles between us. We only had limited time to gossip because spying and trying to come up with some sort of plan took hours. Really, this seemed like the only normal thing that ever happened to me anymore, and I craved my short time with Lizzie.

"Your sister is kind of a badass; you know that? It's like she's a mini you even though you grew up in Shitsville."

"Isn't she, though? I'm so proud of that kid. I think she was kind of asking me permission a few days ago before she started. She told me about how she used to create profiles on weird fetish sites — some way she could never be tracked. She's got a creep radar too, and it works over the internet. She'd start talking to the really weird ones, you know, the ones that want photos of your feet made up like an ice cream sundae or some shit.

"She's not just a hacker and evil genius, she's good at Photoshop too. She'd send them all the fucked-up photos they wanted, but they were all her creation. She'd start charging them for the more fucked up photos they wanted with the promise she'd eventually come on cam. The little runt came up with that plan after our mother cut her allowance after their cell phone provider charged them this huge fee from Ariel's phone. Apparently, when they said unlimited data, they didn't mean quite that much."

"Why did she get mad at Ariel and not the cell phone company? She pays for unlimited data, and she should get unlimited data."

"I know, right? Punish the runt because Verizon can't keep up with her. She earned way more than her allowance scamming creeps. Odelia noticed she was up and stuck her head in the bedroom while Ariel was taking a break to run to the bathroom. She didn't lock the screen, and Odelia saw the messages. Ariel compared her reaction to the apocalypse."

"It's a genius plan, but she's too young to be talking to Mattan and Drake. It's not just that she's seventeen and they are older. They are beasts from the bible and Ariel can't even vote yet."

"I know. Ariel and I were texting. I'm going to take over talking to Mattan and Drake, so the peace is kept. Ariel will be researching beasts and the apocalypse since everything is fucked up because Mattan forced it early."

That was actually part of a solid plan, and so far, we were slim on those. "You and Natalia seemed close. How was your date?"

"Oh, Tabby, there was wine, candles, and a private table. A man came out with a violin and played music at our table while we ate. It wasn't just the setting. I was laughing all night, and we have so much in common. I had no idea following you here was going to find my family and link me to some sort of biblical prophecy. Don't you think it's weird our mother's little circle of friends has us so connected? You're the Lamb, I'm the witness, and Natalia and I both ended up lesbians?"

"And my twin has a Lizzie fetish and wants to make you his queen. Don't forget that part."

Lizzie groaned. "I'd been trying to block that part out. I wonder if I accidentally brushed those gross kitty balls when I was bathing him and now, he wants me to touch his gross little Antichrist balls."

"You picked him up that first day, remember? You thought he was cute. Maybe he thought you could see the man behind the beast and you're meant to be like a fairy tale."

"Really, Tabby? Are you going to quote that movie? The only thing you liked about that movie was the bad guy."

"Because he had the best songs. I'm just saying; you thought Drake was cute the first day you met him in the cat. Maybe it meant something to him, and now he's gone stalker level two hundred."

"Because that's the luck we have, right?" Lizzie laughed. "It's brought several special weirdos into our lives before, but your twin takes the cake, Tabby. How are things with your Horsemen?"

"I got Bash's pants off," I bragged.

"Is he packing?"

"He was actually trying to prove a point," I pouted. "He kept the thong on to tease me. He definitely may beat you for all those oral skills you always brag about."

"No way," Lizzie said, popping a truffle into her mouth. "Even a bad lesbian has better oral skills than a dude. They don't understand vaginas like a woman."

"You're a vagina snob, Lizzie. Men are perfectly capable of pleasuring a woman with enough practice."

Lizzie wasn't even remotely bi. She only dated girls. When Lizzie was sixteen, she tried to have sex with the guy she was dating and got totally grossed out and left. That was her one and only experience with a man. I was totally bi, but would never experiment with Lizzie. Lizzie was of the opinion only a woman knew how to pleasure another woman. My experience told me there were rotten lovers no matter what gender you identified with.

Lizzie and I had deep, philosophical conversations about this back home. It was mostly on nights when one of us was upset, and we had cheap vodka and a fun-sized bag of M&Ms. If we started that conversation tonight, we'd be up all night. This was at least a nine-hour debate with us. I changed the subject because once Lizzie got started talking about giving oral sex, she talked for hours.

"Are you seeing Natalia tonight?"

"Yes. I'm calling her when I get home, and she's going to show me some movies on Netflix. Who is guarding you tonight?"

"Chase. He—"

"I'm shocked you didn't beg for Chase first. I swear, for a hot minute there, I thought you were going to start masturbating to those *Lord of the Rings* movies instead of porn like a civilized person."

"Oh, come on. That movie is full of hot men. Chase is pretty, isn't he? They are all hot in their own way. I didn't beg for Chase first because I can't pick between them."

"There's two of them you've insulted me by saying they've got better skills than me and you can't pick? Girl, you've got a greedy vagina."

"Well, my greedy vagina has a date with Conquest, and something tells me Natalia doesn't just want to show you movies tonight. You can get over your butthurt at me saying Zed and Bash have better vagina skill than you by making Natalia scream."

Lizzie just grinned innocently at me. "I think Natalia is the type of girl to return the favor."

Chapter 26

Chase apparently really didn't like to wait. Almost as soon as I walked into my bedroom, he pounced. He slammed me against the wall and was passionately kissing me. One hand had my hands clasped above my head, and the other was yanking at my corset laces. I was fairly tall, especially in my boots, but the Horsemen all towered over me. I had a feeling Chase was going to totally dominate me in a way none of the Horsemen had done so far, and I couldn't wait.

I wanted to set him off. I bit his tongue pretty hard. Chase growled and gave my corset laces a hard yank. I reached up and tried to find the strip he used to tie his long, white hair back. I wasn't gentle when I tugged it loose. Chase's hair was even longer than mine and fell in a curtain around my face once I freed it. I was having all kinds of fantasies about running my fingers through that soft hair and pulling it while he fucked the shit out of me.

Chase growled again and picked me up. His face was buried in my neck as he carried me to the bed. "I was hoping corsets would be out of fashion when the seals were broken again. You look delicious in them, but getting women out of them has always been a huge pain in the ass."

"Did you always win when you fought over women, Mister Horseman of Conquest?"

"When I was human, yes. After we were made Horsemen, we didn't get that many opportunities."

"You were human once?" I asked. This was the first I heard about this.

Chase groaned and started tugging on my laces again. "I finally have you to myself with that filthy mouth of yours, and now you want to use it to chat?"

"I expect a full explanation about all of you being human once you're doing showing me what Conquest can do," I said, going to help him with the corset. "I know I won't get your pants off, but will you take your shirt off?"

Chase sat back and grinned at me. "If you'll get that infernal corset off for me, sure, I'll take my shirt off."

I'd learned to get myself in and out of corsets pretty easily and quickly. I peeled the two pieces back and shrugged it off. I laid back on the bed and looked at Chase expectantly.

"Your turn."

It was like Chase's eyes were glowing a little as he stared down at my body. He shook his head like he was trying to clear it and pulled his shirt off. Chase was pale, but not as pale as Bash. They'd explained to me he was the White Rider. I thought that meant his horse, but his hair was long and white and his skin was porcelain. It was a huge contrast with Chase's coloring and the desire in his eyes as he looked down at me.

He looked downright evil for a light elf. "Now that I have you, what shall I do with you, little lamb? What's your favorite?"

"What's your specialty, Conquest? Zed has his fingers and Bash has his tongue. Show me what you're good at," I shot back.

"I wish I could *really* show you Conquest, but we've all agreed no making love to you just quite yet. I've got the perfect thing. One of my favorites and just the thing to make the others feel you've been pleasured by Conquest."

"Oh, really? You going to show me or just brag about it."

"That mouth of yours, Tabitha. I believe you accused me of being a two-pump chump in need of a pity fuck when we first met. I'm so going to enjoy proving that little insult wrong when I finally get to make love to you. Let me show you what the Horseman of Conquest can do even with his pants on."

Chase practically tackled me. I was pinned on my back in an instant. Chase certainly kissed like the Horseman of Conquest. It wasn't deep and passionate like Bash. It was raw and feral, like he was marking me in some way. He bit me several times, and the pinch of his teeth on my lower lip was sending jolts through my body. His hand was so large, it covered my breast entirely. His hand was scorching hot as it massaged and squeezed.

His hand was like this butterfly when he moved it between my legs. He wasn't massaging my clit or fingering me. I didn't know what he was doing other than it felt fucking good. His hand was just fluttering on my clit lightly. It was enough to inflame my body and want more, but Chase didn't want to give it to me just yet. Was this payback for calling him a two-pump chump? I was thrusting my hips up to get more contact, and he would just move his hand away.

"Chase, if I promise to be nicer to you, will you be nicer to me right now?" I begged.

Chase just kept up that flutter. I nearly screamed when I moved my hips towards his hand again, and he moved it away.

"Ah, Tabby, be your regular sarcastic self. I don't want you to change. This is not revenge or torture. This is just part of a much bigger plan."

"Care to clue me in on the plan?"

Chase stopped his attention on my neck and started sucking on my nipple. "No, because it ruins the surprise. I can feel you're turned on and pissed at the same time. It's nice being with someone I'm connected to in some weird way. Trust I can feel you and know exactly what you can and can't handle."

I tried to focus on anything but wanted Chase to give me more than that little flutter. I heard them once, and they could feel me somehow. Could I feel them? I tried to remember what I was feeling the first time I heard their thoughts. I had to not think about it too hard and relax. I focused on all four of them. What made them different, the little things that drove me nuts about all of them.

That was when I felt it. It hit me like a tidal wave. I could feel Chase. Teasing me like this had him aroused. He wanted to fuck me just as much as I wanted him to. It gave him pleasure to watch me squirm, but he really wanted to hold me down and give me the fucking of my life. And all this time, I thought they all just had exceptional control.

They did, just a little less than I was thinking. Zed, Gideon, and Bash were all in their bedrooms jerking off because they could feel me. They were taking their time because Chase was taking his time with me. I could sense them all slowly stroking their cocks. I just couldn't see anything. I bucked and moaned when I felt the pleasure from all of them,

Chase totally stopped his fluttering and looked at me proudly. "I was hoping if I did that enough and gave you a hint, you'd explore your connection with us. It goes both ways, you know. I felt you get even more aroused. Did you finally feel the connection?"

"Oh god," I moaned. "I can still feel it, and you aren't even touching me anymore. I can feel Zed, Bash, and Gideon touching themselves and I can feel how turned on you are."

Chase chuckled. "Hold on to that feeling, Tabby. I'm conducting an experiment and trying to make a point. I want you to fuck my face now, but I want you to focus on what you're feeling and what everyone else is feeling too."

Chase grabbed me and rolled us so that I was straddling his face. My eyes rolled back into my head when I felt him fucking me with his tongue. The sensations I was getting from Zed, Bash, and Gideon got stronger, and I knew I was in for a hell of a night tonight. Chase was even more turned on with me sitting on his face.

Chase and I both lost control. Chase's arms clamped over my thighs as he furiously licked my clit. I was grinding my pussy into his tongue and enjoying sensations from all around me. I'd never had sex like this before. I could feel Chase's tongue bringing me to a fast, intense orgasm, but I could feel the others getting close too.

It was too much for me. I just sort of exploded all over Chase. I'd never come that hard in my entire life. I shrieked loud enough to wake the entire house, but I also felt Zed, Bash, and Gideon come *with* me. I felt more than my orgasm, and my entire body was shaking.

Chase didn't even give me a chance to recover. He pulled me down to his chest and just laughed. Bash told me what he found so funny, but Chase was laughing like he just took over a country. Damned Horseman of Conquest.

"Well, that solves that little mystery," he chuckled. "And when Gideon gets that stick out his ass and agrees, we are going to give you the fivesome of your life. I need to get in the shower."

"Seriously? You're just going to give me an orgasm like that, talk about a mystery being solved, and not even stay to cuddle with me and talk about it?"

"Tabby, the big mystery with if we're going to die is solved. We're all connected to you in some way, or we *all* wouldn't have come with you just now. I need to take a shower because I made a mess, understand? Gideon kept insisting this was some illusion Drake was pulling making you think you wanted all of us and making us think we wanted you. We'd act on it, and you'd be alone. Gideon can't deny the connection anymore. You can hear us and feel us the same way we do each other. Clearly, you've been suggesting all those filthy things, and we haven't been able to control ourselves around you for a reason."

"But what does it all mean, Chase?"

Chase just shrugged. "I've got no idea why we are connected this way. We can snuggle and talk theories when I get out the shower."

CHAPTER 27

Breakfast was super awkward. I thought now that we were all connected, things would be easier. None of them would look at me, and it was like they were blocking their thoughts from me. It was like when you just intended to have a one-night stand, and you accidental passed the fuck out all night. You wake up at the same time as some dude whose name you don't know, and they ask if you want breakfast. They don't *really* want to feed you, and you just want to get the hell out of dodge, but you stay and eat anyway, so you don't hurt feelings. That was my breakfast.

And I wasn't having it. Normally I just slunk home after I ate, but I had something deeper with the Four Horsemen. "Okay, someone had better start talking and explain why shit just got awkward."

"It's several things, Tabby," Gideon sighed. Out of all of them, he was always the one to explain, even if it was hard or may hurt my feelings. He always tried to soften the blow and explain it in a way that I could understand or make it better for me. I appreciated that from Gideon, even if he sometimes seemed suspicious of me. "We don't know what you are or why you're connected to us in this way. We don't know if it means we die, you die too. This is the way it's been for us every time we are released. We all die at the same time. Being connected like this doesn't just mean the sex you are wanting. It could mean you are in danger *from* us because of the connection. This could be a trick from Drake. I still haven't ruled that out."

"No, it's not Drake," I argued. "Drake needs me alive to break the rest of the seals. He needs you alive for the apocalypse. Drake can't have his new heaven or earth without the five of us. Drake and Mattan probably have no idea what happened to the Horsemen after the seals had been broken even to create an elaborate ruse like this. Whatever this is, its not Drake and Mattan."

"She's right," Bash pointed out. "No one but us and the angel that connected us this way would know what happened to us the few times the seals were broken. Whatever is happening to Tabby and the rest of us, it's not an illusion from Drake. What we all feel from her is very real."

"Chase said you used to be human. Tell me about that and the connection," I said.

"It was different times. A very long time ago when humans were still primitive. We didn't know each other as humans. This was a very long time before the original tribes your families came from," Zed explained. "We were from different tribes across the world. We didn't even have religion, really. We just knew hunting and surviving. We did have culture of our own. We fought wars, took over other tribes, and had our own systems of justice, even if we were primitive.

"All of us died for the good of our tribes, saving lives, defeating evil. We died at different times. We all got to Heaven at different points in time, but we were chosen. We were gathered together and spoken to by a white light without a face. It explained the destiny it was offering us and what was to come. The light never said anything about you or the connections we have. That was something we figured out on our own.

"We were held in a sort of purgatory of sorts. It was a separate part of heaven maybe. It changed as the years changed so we could stay up to date on Earth technology. We were given training on how to carry out the apocalypse when it finally came. Twenty-six years ago, we were approached by another white light. We were told about Mattan forcing the apocalypse. It was not the right time.

"We were only supposed to get involved if the seals broke. We weren't told anything about you at all, but we were given a lot of information on Drake. Heaven didn't get involved because smiting people in this day and age has different ramifications than the old day and you and Drake had only just been conceived. It was decided just to wait and see what happened."

"What the fuck?" I demanded. "You find out Mattan, who is possibly one of the beasts in the Book of Revelations has just raped my mother and created *The* Beast and you just wanted to wait and hope everything turned out okay?"

Chase put his hand over mine. "The Horsemen aren't angels, Tabby. We're weapons. We don't have wings or various angelic gifts. We have a purpose and a job, and we are given just enough information to do it. We're soldiers on a mission when we are on Earth. It's like we're in the middle of a dead zone and can't get orders. We've never known why we are connected this way, and we have no way of asking what's going on with you."

Bash was chewing on his bottom lip. "Clearly, when we were told the angels were just going to wait and see what happened, something went on in the background. Heaven got involved with Tabby. It makes sense, don't you see? Tabby is not just the Lamb. She's been given the ability to blow Drake to the Lake of Fire. Tabby has been made a weapon of Heaven too. She wasn't asked or given a choice like we were, but she's technically a weapon now. It's the superpowers she keeps talking about."

Gideon started nodding. "I think you're onto something. We're weapons of the Apocalypse. Tabby was made one too to stop Drake and Mattan because it's not the time for the apocalypse yet. *That's* why we're all connected. We're all different parts of the same weapon."

Well, wasn't that the shit? It was kind of like finding out I was a clone or an alien or something. Some angel just went right in and gave me the power to super burp without my permission. I'd rather be Spiderman. He's got cool powers. All I could do was blow on people and send them to hell.

Was it something I had to learn to control? Like, would I be out of breath blowing up balloons for a party and send the entire room to hell? What a lame power. Sure, it could stop Drake, but what the hell was I supposed to do with it after Drake? I couldn't break it out at parties to impress people.

Zed looked concerned. "You've got that look on your face again like you're about to explode."

"You said Mattan would be punished. Do you have something better for him than me just blowing him to hell? Because I didn't ask for any of this. I'm glad I met the four of you, but I never asked to be a weapon, and Lizzie and Ariel never asked to blow fire out their mouths and be witnesses either."

"As the Horseman of Justice, I have access to hell. I can create Mattan his own personal hell, and you can send him there. Drake will burn for all eternity in the Lake of Fire," Zed said.

"I have a question," I said. I had a million questions, but I'd settle for one right now. "If I send the Antichrist to the Lake of Fire when Heaven is finally ready for their little apocalypse, are they going to get a Rothledge and a Lamb together to just make a new one? I kind of feel like Heaven's recycling right now."

"Sofa, now," Chase ordered.

I hardly had time to think. Zed scooped me up and carried me to the sitting room. Before I knew it, I was sitting in Chase's lap getting a shoulder rub, and Zed had my boots off rubbing my feet. They knew all my weak spots. Bastards.

"You would be sending *one* Antichrist to the lake. There is the potential for an Antichrist in every generation just like every child born to the Lambs has the potential to break the seals. You aren't recycled. Think of it like an inheritance. A blood right," Gideon tried to explain.

"Most people inherit a little money and old jewelry," I grumbled. "If I'm now a weapon, does that mean I just die after I defeat Drake? Am I *always* going to be a weapon and have to fight again when the actual apocalypse happens?"

Chase kissed my neck. "Would it be so bad being in a huge manor like this in a private area of heaven for all eternity with all of us?"

"There's no fucking in Heaven. We'd just be weapons, doing our celestial jobs."

Bash started laughing. "There is totally fucking in heaven. What do you think married couples in heaven do? We've all had sex in heaven."

"Okay, so I'm a weapon, and I may die when this is over. No one is giving me a get out of jail free card. Do we actually have a plan to stop Drake yet?"

Zed started rubbing my calves. "We have time to deal with Drake. We have all feel you're upset, Tabby. You didn't ask for this, and you weren't asked permission like we were. Before we deal with Drake, I want you to think up a special hell for Mattan. I'll create it, and you can send him there. I think revenge on Mattan will give you closure once all this is done."

Zed was right. If I ended up dying and going to some private Heaven with my Horsemen because I was now one of Heaven's weapons, I'd feel a lot better about it if I knew my stupid father was in a hell I made up for him.

I was going to need Lizzie to create the perfect hell for Mattan. I could come up with something pretty twisted on my own, but Lizzie was chatting with him about all his perverted sexual fantasies. I was going to turn Mattan's escort visits against him, and he was never getting laid again.

CHAPTER 28

I never believed in fate or destiny before. The way I grew up, I just seemed stupid to believe in that. It would mean someone or something put me in that fucked up situation for a reason. Well, fuck me, it totally did. Fate continued to fuck with me, and I decided I'd rather have a destiny like Harry Potter and fight Voldemort and an army of Deatheaters than my entire purpose was just to blow Drake to hell and die. No one could tell me if we were all just going to up and die when this was done. It seemed like *someone* should be able to answer that for me if they were just going to make me a weapon.

When everyone found out we were making our move once I figured out Mattan's punishment, everyone got involved, and Esther insisted on calling my grandparents. She thought they needed to know about my new status as a weapon and should give input on Mattan. It was going to be super awkward coming up with a sexual torture hell for Mattan in front of my damned grandparents, but super awkward was becoming my norm.

Lizzie had only just started chatting with Mattan and Ariel had more input on his sick fantasies. Apparently, he didn't record his escort visits like Drake did, so we had no idea what twisted things Papa Dearest was into. Odelia just scowled at Ariel as she spilled all Mattan's kinky secrets, but didn't make a scene again.

"So, he likes them barely eighteen and blonde, right? I'm talking like, turned eighteen a month ago. If he could hire a minor, he totally would. He's into degrading women. He positions himself like a Dom in chat, but the way he phrases things, he's not a real Dom. It's not a respectful relationship with a submissive. He's just a bully."

"Explain, runt," Lizzie said. Natalia was here with us again, and I could tell Lizzie was desperately in love. So was Natalia. The two of them were practically glued together on the sofa.

"He wants to do things like spitting, choking, and pissing on someone without building up trust first. He just wants some girl barely out of high school to come over and do all that on the first visit. Some people are into that, but Mattan isn't looking for those people. He uses escorts because he wants to hurt women that aren't all that comfortable with it, but do it because they are getting paid."

"The kid is right," Gideon said. "I'm into the escort services computers now. Mattan pays them a lot of money to send women who fit his personal preference with no warning about where his proclivities lie. Most of the girls they send to him, he's their first visit because their regulars are too old for him. It's not a respectable service. They don't respect their workers, or they would have dropped Mattan after the first complaint."

I remembered what Lizzie said about Ariel being a whiz on Photoshop. "Ariel, do you think you could whip up Mattan's perfect girl in Photoshop?"

That kid had to be a borderline genius in nearly every way imaginable. I hoped when all this was over, even if I died, Lizzie and Ariel got to live out their lives. Lizzie deserved some happiness and Ariel was going to do great things. I could already tell. With her ability at extorting perverts, I thought she'd be perfect for Speaker of the House one day.

I was coming up with a plan for Mattan. He'd get his young blonde fantasy, but he'd never get to touch her. She'd be with him for all eternity taunting him about his failures. She'd be reminding him every day he was there because *I* created this hell for him. I remembered the portraits in my parent's bedroom. There would be portraits of me posing like a badass on every wall in his hell.

Mattan liked to degrade and cause pain, but he probably didn't like being on the receiving end of it. I decided for the final torture, a new girl would come in every night. She would get his hopes up he was getting laid. She'd let him say horrible things to her, but as soon as he went to act on his sexual fantasies, he'd find himself strapped to a bed. He would be the one getting spat on and choked. His little raping dick would never get attention. I decided this would go on for hours before the girl left a big steaming dump on his chest and disappeared.

He'd have to stay chained to the bed with a big pile of shit on his chest while his perfect woman taunted him from across the room reminded him he created this mess in the first place by being a raping douchebag and hurting girls. I felt like I was leaving something out. Something important.

My Oma was the one that spoke. She hadn't said a single word about my hell for Mattan. She hadn't said I was some sick, twisted child who needed to be committed. She didn't tell me I went too far. She just nodded at me.

"He hurt your mother too. I know Drake killed them. To complete your hell, you need portraits of her down there too."

That was the missing piece. Zed's superpowers were that he could just blink and create Mattan's hell for me. Now, we just needed to get Drake and Mattan in front of us to send them straight to hell.

CHAPTER 29

The best plan I could come up with that everyone agreed with was to invite Drake and Mattan over for dinner. I would talk to Drake telepathically and tell him there were things I needed to air out with both him and Mattan before I would hear him out about breaking any more seals. Gideon didn't think it would work, but I still thought there was a part of Drake that wanted a twin sister. He had to have been lonely in that cat, and I just had to bank on that.

Lizzie did something I tried to talk her out of. I didn't want her anywhere near Drake or Mattan. She told me to tell Drake she wanted to be there if I sensed doubt from him. I was supposed to tell my brother that my very lesbian best friend finally saw a photo of him and had a great conversion to straighthood and wanted to jump on his dick.

"Lizzie, no one is going to believe that!"

Lizzie gave me one of her famous snorts. "Your twin will. You forget, he went straight to the Incels before Mattan started buying him friends. The idea the woman he wants for his queen no longer wants women because she saw his photo is going to go straight to his tiny little Incel brain. He'll come here no matter what Mattan says because he thinks he's getting laid. Mattan will come with him because he knows that story is bullshit and we're up to something."

I looked at my four Horsemen. I started this not catching the seals when Drake swatted them off the desk. Lizzie and Ariel were in danger just because I had been born. All of these people that had crashed into my life, my mother's friends, my grandparents, my Horsemen, they were in danger from my twin and my father. And I was inviting them both for dinner. I knew no matter what I said, they would all want to be hiding in the house somewhere.

"Is there a weapon anywhere that can hurt any of you?" I asked the Horsemen.

"Horseman perk," Chase said, winking at me. "It's a perk you have too. Since we *are* weapons, there's nothing on Earth that can kill us. We'll be hiding with our weapons in case Drake or Mattan try anything, but you and Lizzie have weapons of your own. Don't let them bully you."

"Like Tabby and I would *ever* let a man bully us," Lizzie snorted.

Bash got the giggles again. "Remember, you can blow them both to hell before you go threatening to put your boot up their asses."

"Please," I said, holding up my hand. "I can't fly, and I can't go invisible like all the cool superheroes. If I'm blowing someone to hell, they aren't leaving without a witty retort from me, and it's going to be so much better than my boot up their ass."

I wondered if Gideon found anything funny at all. "Don't hesitate with them, Tabby. Don't give them a moment to escape by coming up with something sarcastic to send them off with. Just blow them straight to hell and get it over with."

"You are absolutely no fun at all Gideon."

Maybe Gideon did have a sense of humor. And brass balls to comment on his in front of my grandparents. "We've been putting off your kinky little fantasies until Drake was dealt with. If you don't waste time with silly speeches that may allow them to escape, we can finally do what we've all been wanting."

I hadn't even thought about my fivesome with the Horsemen since I found out I was a weapon and could die. If there were any fairness in the world at all, I'd go out right at the end of hot sex with all four of them. The world couldn't totally fuck me out of everything, right?

CHAPTER 30

Lizzie was right. It was official. The Antichrist was a horny Incel that immediately bought the story that the one lesbian he wanted was willing to convert to dick just because she saw a photo and thought he was hot. I thought the Antichrist was supposed to be cunning and smart. He seemed suspicious, but after I fed him Lizzie's story, he turned from Antichrist to fourteen-year-old virgin with his first crush.

It was just so wrong fielding all the questions from my twin asking about my very lesbian best friend's interest in him. To be honest, Lizzie was so pissed about him ignoring the fact that she wasn't into men at all and still wanted her for his queen, I wouldn't put it past her to set him on fire on sight. I hadn't seen Lizzie use her dragon breath before, but she did like to show off and blow smoke circles. She'd even mastered smoke hearts and blew them around Natalia to show off.

Could she set two men on fire at once? Both Mattan and Drake had gotten creepy with her. Me and the Horsemen and planned for this. If Lizzie just started setting people on fire, there would be flaming swords and bows at the Horsemen's disposal to slow anyone down from running so that I could blow them to hell.

I had to do a lot of ass kissing to get Drake here. Mattan had to know we were up to something and was trying to talk Drake out of coming. He kept contacting me telepathically needing reassurance that Lizzie was going to be there and really was into him. I tried sweetening the pot by trying to have Drake's favorite foods prepared.

I tried not to laugh like a maniac when I asked Drake what his favorite food was and he told me tuna. Of course, it was tuna. Those treats that got him out from under the bed when he was still a cat were tuna treats. Didn't he just go nuts trying human food once he was a real boy again and have something other than fish he liked? I just pictured him in his sad, pretend Goth clothes eating canned tuna and jerking off to his escort visits. I knew the Antichrist was supposed to be evil, but Drake was this sad little pervert who believed lesbian fairy tales.

I had a dinner created and waiting to be served on the patio. Everyone was hiding when our butler let Drake and Mattan through the front door. Mattan was dressed in an expensive three-piece suit, and Drake was dressed like someone who was trying to pretend to be Goth for a costume party. It was too overboard, like a parody of being Goth. I was polite, and thankfully, Lizzie didn't set anyone on fire as we led them to the backyard. Lizzie even took Drake's arm like she was totally into him. Drake was actually giggling like a girl that Lizzie was touching him.

Dinner was served, and it was under the pretense of me hearing Mattan out. Bash convinced me to listen to him before I blew him to his private hell. He thought Mattan might say something to give me closure about everything he had done and everything that had happened to me since I got here. Really, I just wanted to give him an epic verbal smackdown and use my lame superpower to send him to hell, but I got outvoted by every single Horseman, my grandparents, and even Lizzie betrayed me on this one.

Mattan had his oily eyes and smiles out tonight instead of the trusting man that got me here. He placed his napkin into his lap daintily. "So, Tabitha, what is the real reason we are here tonight?"

"The same reason I told Drake. You have a lot to answer for. You raped my mother, and you've been lying to me from the start. If you expect me to participate in your little apocalypse, you'd better start explaining. I'm the only one who can break the seals, and I control the Horsemen. You went through all this trouble to start this, but you can't complete it without me. Why should I follow you after everything?"

"There are a lot of reasons. Think about it, Tabitha. Your parents could have had me thrown in jail, but they didn't. Instead, they chose to keep you secret. If they had pressed charges, I would have been in jail and couldn't have come near you or Drake anyway. Your parents could have raised you right and prevented all of this. If they hadn't sent you to that horrible situation in Kentucky, they could have prepared you not to break the seals. If they had been loving parents to Drake instead of cursing him into a cat, Drake might not have even wanted to try to trick you into starting the apocalypse. You seem to be under the impression I raped your mother to start this. It didn't happen that way. I got drunk at one of their parties and made a serious mistake. I was the one who made a horrible mistake. Your parents were the ones who wronged both you and Drake."

Maybe some of my new superpowers weren't totally useless. I couldn't just get into Drake's mind and the Horsemen. Maybe being a weapon wasn't totally lame. I could read Mattan's mind too, and he didn't even know. Mattan was lying straight to my face, and I could already tell he'd fed Drake this story. Drake seemed to believe it and didn't question it because he tried to defend Mattan to me.

"Mattan has been a *real* father to me since I sensed he was my father the first time he was back in the house. Elliot never liked me. Our mother made my sweaters and gave me my baths, but she never played with me after she stuck me in the cat. I was like a nuisance for both of them. Mattan is showing me what real family is like and I want my twin back. Everyone Elliot and Levana wronged can be together again and heal. We have a destiny. Elliot and Levana tried to stop it, but we are meant to rule the new heaven and earth. It's been written."

Now was the time for epic speeches and a little blowing to hell. Mattan was lying, and Drake was delusional.

"Mattan, you're lying to me, and you lied to Drake too," I said softly.

"Young lady, perhaps you don't know what it's like to have a real father, but you can't just accuse me of lying. You will respect me."

I threw back my head and just laughed like I was totally insane. Mattan was just as delusional as Drake. I didn't respect *anyone* until they earned it. It got me into a lot of trouble in school, but it wasn't getting me in trouble now.

"Calm yourself, Tabitha!" Mattan snapped. "I'm your father, and Drake wants to be a family again. You're ruining everything!"

"Oh, Papa Dearest, you have no idea what you released when you raped my mother, do you?" I purred. I was going to play with Mattan a little. The nerve. Coming to *my* house, lying to me, then demanding my respect just because he was my sperm donor?

The Horsemen warned me. I should have listened. Mattan came armed. He moved fast. He grabbed Lizzie and had a gun pointed to her head before I could send him to hell. Drake was yelling at Mattan about hurting his queen. Mattan was looking at both of us with this frightening, deathly calm.

"Lizzie means *nothing* to me and is just going to cause problems. Lizzie means everything to you. So, let's play a little game, Tabitha. You tell me what you're really up to and Lizzie will live as Drake's plaything. You can continue to disrespect me, and I'll just put a bullet in her pretty head and force you to open the seals."

A flaming arrow flew across the yard and knocked the gun from Mattan's hands. My Horsemen promised me they would keep Lizzie safe and they were certainly keeping that promise. Lizzie whirled to face Mattan. Her eyes were glowing this eerie blue.

"You *did not* just hold a gun to my head and threaten to give me to your son. Did you research the witnesses at all, shit head?"

Lizzie blew this stream of fire out her mouth that would have rivaled any movie dragon. It didn't kill Mattan, but it looked like it hurt like hell. I could smell burning flesh and hear the sounds of his screams. No one had really trained me on the breath of God because if I used it, I'd just blow people to hell.

I had no idea what I was doing. I blew in Mattan's general direction. If someone were just watching our crazy dinner party, it would look like Mattan caught fire and I was trying to blow him out like a candle because I was a total idiot. I felt something stirring inside me. I just pursed my lips and blew, but what came out of me was this swirling white light. It came out like a shotgun blast, and when it hit Mattan, he just disappeared.

I turned to make sure Drake hadn't run. I'd never get him back in my sights if he saw what I could do. I grinned when Drake totally looked like he was going to shit himself with Gideon's flaming sword at his neck.

"Tabby, please. Mattan lied to me too. I had no idea he would try to hurt Lizzie when he knows I love her. I can't help how I was born, Tabby. Help me."

I walked over to Drake. I could sense the real truth from him. "Your power is deception, Drake. You would have sensed Mattan was lying to you. You chose to believe his story because it fits your agenda. I know about the Incels and the man you're trying to get to be your prophet. You knew Mattan wasn't telling you the full truth about raping our mother. You can blame our parents all you want, but they were young and scared. You chose to follow Mattan when Mattan was the one who made you what you are. Mattan did all this to force the apocalypse, and it's not time yet. You followed him because you *wanted* to and you like the idea of ruling Heaven and Earth. Your power may be deception, but I've picked up a few superpowers of my own."

"What did you do to Mattan, Tabby? You're ruining everything!" Drake said, stamping his foot like a child. "Call off your Horseman and bring Mattan back. I was hoping we could do this as a family without me having to force you to break seals again."

I got right up in Drake's pasty face. "Maybe you don't realize the power dynamic here, twin. The Horseman of War has a flaming sword at your neck, and you aren't getting *anything* you want."

"The Horsemen can't kill me. There's only one thing that can kill me. You won't stop me, Tabitha. I'll eventually get my army. I'll come back. You'll open the seals and Lizzie will be mine."

I laughed. Maybe my new superpowers weren't totally lame. I was having fun with this. "The one thing that can kill you just sent Mattan to a special hell of the Horseman of Justice's making. When Mattan decided to force the apocalypse, I was made a weapon of Heaven. Guess who has the power to kill you, Drake?"

There was no fear in Drake's eyes. He no longer looked like some sad little pervert. He looked like sheer evil that didn't care he had a flaming sword at his neck and I could kill him. He hardly moved, but suddenly, he just wasn't there anymore. What the fuck was this? I went to step forward and I felt myself being yanked off balance. If that fucker could turn invisible and all I got was super breath, I was going to be upset.

I felt myself falling. Was Drake sending *me* to hell? Maybe not. I landed on a rug and all the air was knocked out my lungs. Drake was on me in seconds. His knees were pressed on my chest and I could hardly breathe. He had one hand around my throat and the other covering my mouth and nose. I could breathe, but barely.

"How appropriate that this happens here and now. Look around you. This was my nursery before our mother cursed me. I brought you to right before she stuck me in that cat. Mattan thought I could do this, but I didn't think it was needed. I *hoped* you'd feel sorry for me for what our mother did to me. You're just a bitch like her.

"I don't need you. I can kill you now and change history. I just have to destroy Levana's little hex book and plant a few delusions in her head that we are a totally happy family. I'll never end up in that cat and when I get older, I'll eventually meet Mattan. You'll be on my side then. You'll break the seals like we need and it won't come to this.

"I'll find my two-year-old self and whisper in his ear what Levana had planned for us. I'm not going to kill her now, but when I'm old enough, I will. I don't want her giving you any ideas. Think you can kill me? Think again, Tabby. I'm the Antichrist and I'm destined to win. I'm tired of your shit and now it's time for you to die."

My weapon was my breath and now Drake had taken away all ability to breathe. I was starting to see spots and I couldn't force him off my chest. I saw something, someone through the haze of ever-expanding black dots in my vision. Was it an angel come to save me? Drake collapsed on top of me in a heap and I could finally breathe again.

I shoved him off me and tried to see who stopped him. I was looking at my very shocked mother.

"Tabitha?" she asked with wide, tearful eyes. "So, our fears are true. Has the apocalypse started?"

Then, it hit me. Why everything had happened to me. Why they had someone watch me, but never came and got me. Why Drake ended up in the cat. It all had to happen this way to get us to this point and I was here for a reason. Drake had no idea what he was doing bringing me back here and what events he was setting in motion. He'd always blamed our mother when he should have been blaming me. It was like that sci-fi show I loved. *This had happened before.*

I blew at Drake. The swirling white light hit his knocked-out form. Levana had gotten him with a lamp. The Antichrist wasn't immune to getting knocked the fuck out by a copper lamp. Now that Drake was gone, I turned to my mother.

"Listen. I don't know how much time I have here. Things have to happen a certain way *now* to stop the apocalypse. You have to send me away. Use the orphanage the elders use. No matter what you hear or see, you can never contact me. You have a book. You will have to use dark magic and neutralize Drake.

"If Drake remains human, when he's old enough, he will find Mattan and they will find me. They will hurt you and use me. If Drake is put into an animal, it's going to make him a weak Antichrist. He'll become bitter and only focused on certain things. We need Drake this way when I come back because it will make him easier to manipulate."

"Can this be done without sending you away? I could prepare you and you are such a sweet baby."

"You won't be able to keep me a secret any other way. When Mattan finds out about me, he will try to manipulate me. We *have* to keep Mattan and Drake apart for as long as possible. It's going to be hard for everyone, but it has to happen this way, or the apocalypse may happen very differently when I'm old enough. And be careful of Drake when you put him into the cat. Be wary of him trying to trip you."

"The cat? You mean the kitten we got for you to play with? That was meant to be *your* pet."

My parents got me a bat eared, hairless cat as a playmate when I was two? That was new. I could feel myself starting to fall again. Whatever magic Drake had used to get me here was starting to slip and I was going back to my time. I only had to hope I had said the right thing and when I got back, things weren't totally changed.

There was one last thing that needed to be said. I yelled it as I felt myself falling. "Whatever you do, don't put this in any of your videos. Don't record another video after tonight. Mattan will see."

CHAPTER 31

Time travel really should be done in blue police boxes. I saw stars again when I slammed back into the ground in the garden. I heard Lizzie shriek, then she pounced on me. Zed practically yanked me away from her and had me in this huge bear hug.

"I was searching all of hell for you. What happened? Where did you go?"

"Where is Drake? I see his handprints on your neck, Tabitha. I'll show him what a flaming sword feels like," Gideon growled.

"Drake tried to bring me back in time to kill me. How come none of you knew he could do that before I invited him to dinner? He nearly killed me before Levana broke a lamp over his head."

"Wait, your future self met your mother in the past? Isn't shit like that supposed to cause the apocalypse on its own?" Lizzie asked.

"No, all of this, Drake being put in the cat and me ending up in Kentucky was because *I* told her to do it just now. It hit me then. Think about it. Drake would have been much more different and powerful if he grew up human and managed to get in contact with Mattan. It's because he got stuck in that cat for so long, he turned into a whiney little pervert. Drake intended to kill me and change the past and I could have, but I just knew things had to be exactly as they were because it made Drake weaker and made me stronger."

I was suddenly surrounded by this mass group hug. Gideon was back to playing with my hair.

"Oh, Tabby. So, the only memory you have of your mother now is you telling her to send you away?" Gideon asked.

Did they think I was breakable? I liked the group hug, but I wasn't looking at this the same way they were. I rubbed my face in Zed's chest. They didn't need a sarcastic answer. They needed to know I was okay.

"No. My memory of my mother is her saving my life and us working together to stop Drake. She had no idea. She had been watching us. She helped me by knocking him out and I helped her by keeping Mattan away. I tried to warn her about Drake and stairs, but I don't think I could have prevented her death."

"I'm glad you see it that way, Tabby," Chase said, rubbing my arms.

Feelings were gross and I had them all over me. I needed to know this was done and I'd stopped Drake and Mattan. I'd already had one surprise tonight with Drake's little time travel trick, I didn't want another one.

"Zed, you have access to hell. Did it work?" I asked. "Is Mattan in his personal hell and Drake in the Lake of Fire?"

"Let me show you something, Tabby," Zed said. He placed his palm on my forehead. I could see what he saw in hell.

Mattan was indeed in the room Zed created, but he hadn't realized it yet. He was pounding on the walls demanding to be let out. He actually pulled the *do you know who I am* line. The young blonde hadn't let herself be seen yet. My little torturer was good at her job. She let Mattan work himself into a rage before she finally came out.

"Welcome to hell, Mattan. Courtesy of your daughter and the Horseman of Justice. We're going to have so much fun with you here."

Mattan let out this primal shriek and tried to destroy one of the paintings of me on the wall. It splintered as he broke it on a chair, then totally disappeared from his hands and reappeared on the wall totally intact.

The vision wavered as Zed took his hand off my forehead. "Was that your idea with the paintings?" I asked.

"It was a little detail I thought about at the last minute. After getting taunted enough that he was there because of you, he was going to eventually go for those paintings. I decided the paintings would just come back every time he destroyed one. He's never getting away from you or your mothers face for the rest of eternity."

I thought about Drake. This entire time, I felt sorry for him. I thought he ended up the way he was because he had been stuck in a cat for so long. Really, the cat shaped the sad little pervert that preached to Incels and creeped on my best friend, but I saw what Drake could have been like if left unchecked when he was trying to choke me to death.

This entire time, I had been thinking if Drake had just been raised in a loving home, he wouldn't be doing any of this. The look in his eyes when he was trying to squeeze the life out of me, I knew that was wrong. Drake could have been raised by Levana and Elliot in the most loving of ways. I could have been his loving twin. He still would have sought out Mattan when he sensed the connection, but things would have been much worse than if he hadn't been stuck in the cat. Drake may have discovered all sorts of awful powers and he would have had the time to build up his following. I could have adored Drake as his sister and he would have used and abused me to get what he wanted.

"Is Drake in the Lake of Fire?"

"For now. Lucifer may take mercy on him even though he failed and let him out and give him a better room. Even Lucifer knows this wasn't supposed to happen yet and take mercy on Drake."

Lizzie grabbed my arm and started dragging me back to the house. "We need to have a celebration party then you need to have kinky sex with the Horsemen."

I realized I hadn't died yet. Drake and Mattan were gone, and I wasn't dead. Maybe it was the whole death vagina thing, and it would happen when we had sex. I didn't want to die, but I was starting to accept my life had a greater purpose now. Ariel said there were four beasts in the bible. I sent two to hell today, but I knew if this were the right time for the apocalypse, I never would have gotten that close that easily. If I had to do this again,

I would need to prepare. If I had to die at twenty-six to do that, I'd at least be with my Horsemen.

CHAPTER 32

So, apparently, after I led Mattan and Drake to the backyard, my mother's best friends and my grandparents snuck downstairs to plan an Apocalypse Party. I wasn't even out there that long, and they'd managed to gather all the elders that helped us and some of my extended family I hadn't met yet. There was a full spread of food and flowing booze. Where the hell did they get those decorations and manage to put them up in so little time?

One would think my mother's best friends and my grandparents would throw a rather stuffy party, but I was having a blast. If this was my last night on Earth, this party was a great way to go out. I met so many cousins from my mother's side of the family and a few from Elliot's. There were no Adlers at the part, and for that, I was grateful. If I didn't die, I was thinking of taking my mother's last name, but I wanted to deny any connection to the Adlers.

The elders weren't letting Mattan's crimes go unpunished either. They were digging into the entire Adler family to see if any more plots or crimes were going on we needed to know about.

It was a little surreal seeing so many elders getting drunk and cutting up and I'd just blown air out my mouth and sent two people to hell. I wondered if I'd actually lost it and this had all been a dream when my drunk Oma *climbed on the table* and wanted to give a toast to me. I totally figured out where I got my drunken behavior from because my Oma seemed to love everything when she was drunk too. I hoped she didn't break something trying to get off the table.

I literally just sat there with my mouth open when a crowd gathered by the table and turned into some mosh pit. My Oma just handed her drink to someone, yelled she loved me, then turned and dove into the crowd. They caught her and carried her to the edge of people, then gently set her down.

After everything I'd seen so far, watching my drunk Oma dive into a mosh pit of elders had to be the most bizarre. The elders were a rowdy bunch when they were drunk. My cousins who were around my age were much more behaved than these people who were supposed to be responsible for doling out wisdom.

I was just chilling on the sofa with the Horsemen watching the elders misbehave. I leaned over to Gideon. "Are all the parties here like this?"

"They are celebrating *you,* love. A missing heir who stopped the apocalypse and you brought that orphanage to their attention. You fixed several problems for them in a very short time. You should celebrate too."

I'd always been uncomfortable with praise. This all felt weird, and the room was getting too small. I wanted some fresh air and excused myself to the garden. I sat on a garden wall and just stared at the moon. Suddenly, everything seemed to stand still, and I got this feeling I wasn't alone anymore. I whirled around, ready to fight. I half expected to see Mattan or Drake back from hell, but there was a soft, white light floating in the air.

"You are ill at ease and have questions. We decided you should have answers."

"Who are you?"

"The same angel who extended the offer to your Horsemen. You've done well with the gifts you were given. We should have asked you. We would have, but you were too young. The decision was made the day Drake put the pillow over your face and sat on it. It was dormant until you met the Horsemen."

"Are you normally so cruel to your weapons? You just kill them once they are no longer needed and fall in love. Dying of a broken heart has to be the worse way to die. Are you here to kill me too? Why did you curse them?"

"We didn't curse the Horsemen. Heaven's weapons are not meant to be on Earth for an extended period of time. They always fell for the same woman, but they didn't die of a broken heart. Their time on Earth was just up. They haven't been released that often. It just so happened their time was up at the exact moment every time they were on Earth."

"So, I'm going to die because you made me your weapon. Great gift there, angel."

"Not the way you think. The Horsemen were already dead when they were made weapons. You were and are quite alive. You will live out a normal life until you die naturally, then be called to Heaven as a weapon. And I will tell you something to settle your mind and may make you less angry. The Horsemen are all tied together, and that is why they expire at the same time.

"You are now part of the same weapon as the Horsemen and tied to them. Their time on Earth now matches yours because you all must return at the same time. We have no idea why the five of you seemed to fall in love or use your connection for pleasure, but it doesn't have to end just because you are a weapon. You will have a normal, human life with your family and friends. The Horsemen will get to stay on Earth longer because they are connected to you."

"Did you bind us in other ways? Because I kind of went from wanting to kick them out to wanting to have sex with all of them."

I heard the angel laugh. It sounded like music. "Let's just say heaven wasn't quite expecting the woman you'd grow into anymore than the Horsemen were. That was all you, Tabitha. You did a great thing, Tabitha. You did everything expected of you. Go back inside and celebrate with your friends and family."

The light just winked out, and things seemed to move again. I didn't know what to make of what the angel said. There was no celestial sexual mojo going on that half the time, I was thinking more about my fivesome than the apocalypse. Lizzie was right. I was just a greedy bitch who was easily distracted. And there was never any death vagina stopping our fivesome. Now, I just felt cheated. I could have had them naked this entire time. I'd beaten two beasts. I watched my Oma body surf. It was about time I got my Four Horsemen naked. And they needed the information the angel gave me just as much as I did.

Chapter 33

I finally got the Horsemen up to my bedroom after everyone left and now, they were all shy on me. Before, they wouldn't take their pants off because they were convinced my vagina was going to kill them. Now, they were all nervous about doing this together. They'd never been with a woman all together before or with another man, and they were convinced they were going to hurt me.

"Tabitha, we want to give you what you want, but the idea of hurting you scares us. You're still mortal."

"You aren't going to hurt me, I promise. How about you get naked and if it hurts, I'll tell you to stop? You know I will."

They may have been nervous, but they didn't need that much convincing. They were out their clothes as soon as I promised to tell them to stop. I was *finally* seeing them naked. It was well worth the wait. They all had perfectly sculpted bodies, and it extended to their cocks too. They were standing proud and long and thick enough to have me screaming all night.

Chase made the first move. We were all naked just staring at each other. They were waiting for me to make a move, and I was just standing there like an idiot staring at their beautiful bodies. I thought Chase was going to be rough again and slam me against the wall. I kind of wanted him to. Instead, he just walked over and caressed my cheek.

"That angel should have told you this from the start, Tabby. I'm sorry."

I grabbed his thick cock and started slowly stroking it. It was smooth in my hand. "I think this was like some *Raiders of the Lost Ark* shit for us where it had to be like a quest. They couldn't give us the answer until it was over. If we had known my vagina wasn't going to kill you, we might have been boinking like bunnies instead of stopping Drake and Mattan."

Chase's eyes rolled back in his head. I never expected this from Conquest. "Well, since this was all your idea, how do you want us?"

Four hot Horsemen I could do whatever I wanted with? Oh, I was having so much fun with that. I cocked an eyebrow at them. "Exactly how many rounds can you go?"

Gideon stepped forward being a little, well, not Gideon. "As many as you can handle and then several more," he growled.

"You, down here on the rug," I ordered. "The rest of you come stand around us."

I was slick, and it felt like I had been cockblocked for years from some answer that could have been given to me from the start. Chase was right. Someone could have told me. Now that I had them and I knew no one was going to die, what I had been feeling *needed* to happen finally could.

I remembered that day on the sofa where I came in Gideon's lap without him touching me. Gideon laid on the floor with me, and I climbed on top of him. I knew what *I* wanted to do, but Gideon had other ideas. He flipped me on my back and grinned down at me. His red hair fell in his face again. This time, I brushed it out of his eyes. God, I'd wanted to brush that hair out of his eyes since I met him.

Gideon was relaxed and playful now that the apocalypse was over. His green eyes were practically sparkling. "Everyone has gotten to taste you but me, Tabby. I hardly touched you at all that day I guarded you."

I pulled him down for a deep kiss. Gideon groaned and ground his erection against my stomach. "What do you have planned, War?"

"Hold on tight, little Lamb. I've got skills too. And now that I know I can show them to you, I've got ideas."

I didn't look at the other Horsemen, but I could feel them lazily stroking their cocks while Gideon worshipped my body with kisses. He kissed every inch of my body before nibbling on my knees. Gideon kissed his way up my thighs and gave me this devious look.

"I think I know what you have planned for tonight, so I'll start preparing you now, Tabby."

Gideon lazily circled my clit with his tongue. His fingers slipped inside me and started fingering me, but once they were wet enough, he started working my ass instead. Oh, yes. He knew exactly what I wanted tonight. I could hear the groans of all four men as Gideon lapped at my pussy and started bringing me closer and closer to my orgasm. The thumb of the hand fingering my ass slipped into my pussy. I started grinding against his hand. I was getting close, and I decided to do something stupid. Or maybe not.

"Gideon!" I cried, pulling his hair. They might be able to go all night, but I might not be. "I want to come on your dick."

Gideon pulled back and grinned at me. "You want to drive the Horsemen tonight, but you can't drive any of those cars in the garage?"

"I want to ride your dick for real this time. May I?"

Gideon flopped on his back and yanked me on top of him. "You don't have to ask that twice."

Sliding down Gideon's cock was glorious. It was thick and burned pleasantly as he stretched me out. I finally looked over at the rest of the Horsemen. I had them right where I wanted them.

"I've got a mouth and two hands. Get your asses over here," I ordered.

I heard three growls as they moved forward. I had Chase in my mouth, Bash and Zed were in each hand, and Gideon was buried in my pussy. I was a busy girl. I started grinding against Gideon and working Bash, Zed, and Chase with my hands and mouth. Chase was definitely Conquest because he buried his hands in my hair and started fucking my face. I owed him one anyway. I'd already fucked his.

I thought this would be over quick for all of us. I was turned on as fuck, and I could feel they were too. Gideon was meeting my thrusts and had his head up to bite my nipples. Chase was fucking my face pretty hard; I thought we would all come together like my night with Chase. My orgasm ripped through me, and none of them came. I bucked on Gideon's cock, and my screams were muffled by Chase's in my mouth.

I let go of everyone and threw myself across Gideon's chest panting. My Horsemen no longer seemed shy. They were chuckling now. Gideon wrapped his arms around my waist and gave me a passionate kiss.

"I don't think you quite knew what you were asking for, little lamb. You're still mortal, and we aren't," Gideon chuckled. "We're going to be peeling you off the ceiling for what you want."

I bit Gideon's lip. "So, peel me off the ceiling. And I want a better nickname than little lamb. I'm a weapon, damn it."

CHAPTER 34

I thought I would be giving instructions, but once they helped me stand, Bash came up behind me and started nuzzling my neck. Zed was in front of me with his head bowed nibbling on my nipples.

"When you started suggesting all of us together, we did start watching videos when we could feel you," Bash purred. God, that Horseman had a sexy voice. "I don't think we can do some of the rough stuff in the video, but we can give you what you want."

I reached behind me and started stroking Bash's cock. Zed kissed his way to my mouth and gave me a kiss that took my breath away.

"What do you say, Tabitha? How'd you like to play with Justice and Death? I've got a few ideas," Zed grinned.

"Me too. I've had ideas this entire time. That's why there's lube in the drawer next to my bed," I moaned as Bash bit my ear, "Are you going to tie me up again?"

Zed started making slow circles on my clit. "No, I want you totally free. Bash and I were talking about a video we both watched while you and Gideon were playing."

"Show me," I demanded. "Zed, I owe you for Mattan and Bash I have a feeling I would have owed you if something happened to Lizzie."

Bash gave me a nod. I knew it. If something happened to Lizzie and Ariel, it would have been Bash that brought them back like was promised. I wasn't just doing this because I owed them. We were connected now, bonded. Created as weapons together. We had eternity together. I never wanted to get married, but if I had to spend eternity with someone, these four Horsemen were who I wanted to spend it with.

Zed started walking backward until we all fell on the bed together. I was in a heap with the Horseman of Death and Justice. They'd switched positions. Zed was behind me now, and Bash was kissing me. I felt Zed move to get the lube. Gideon had already done a pretty good job working my ass. Once Zed's fingers were slick, they easily slipped in my ass.

Bash didn't just have skills with his mouth. He was kissing me and making slow circles on my clit as Zed fingered my ass. I was getting close again even with Bash's painfully slow circles. Zed was kissing my neck as he worked my ass. He left a little love bite.

"Do you think you're ready now."

"Oh, god, I'm jumping out my skin. What is this kinky fantasy of yours? I want it, but I don't know if I want you to stop touching me to do it."

I felt Zed leave my back. Bash picked me up and turned me so that I was facing away from Zed. I thought I knew where this was going. Bash guided my ass down Zed's cock. Zed and Gideon had both made sure I was well prepared for this. I let out a contented sigh and leaned back against Zed's chest. I spread my legs and met Bash's eye.

"Is this what you want, Death?"

Bash's eyes were practically feral. "Oh, yeah. And we do need a better nickname of you. Are you ready for me, Tabitha?"

"Get your ass over here, Bash."

When Bash slid into me, I was gloriously filled. They were both long and thick. I was totally stuffed. Just the slightest movement was going to set me off. Zed reached up from underneath me. Oh, that kinky little fuck. He intended to finger me in his position. Zed certainly had skills with his fingers.

Bash started slowly fucking me. Zed had limited movement in this position, and he was fingering me too, but he was still managing to fuck my ass too. Fucking immortals was pretty damned awesome. Bash's eyes never left mine. I could feel Bash and Zed's desire through the link we had as weapons. Bash's eyes were hooded.

"Damn, Tabitha, you feel amazing," Bash growled.

Bash started fucking me harder. I don't know if it was Zed feeling Bash or me, but he started fingering me harder and fucking my ass a little faster. I wanted to see what happened when the Horsemen of Death and Justice went totally out of control. I wanted it hard and rough with them. I was getting fucked by immortals by the first time; I wanted always to remember this even if we had forever to do this again.

"Harder and faster," I ordered. Or begged. I had no idea what I was doing. I was getting fingered and fucked by two Horsemen at once, and I might not be thinking straight.

Bash grabbed my thighs and threw them across his chest. He gripped the top of them, and his eyes rolled back in his head. "You could kill the Horseman of Death; you know that? Let's give her what she wants, Zed."

I had no idea what the hell I was unleashing when I asked two immortal Horsemen to fuck me harder and faster. I was glad the bed was sturdy because it felt like the entire world was shaking. Bash was pounding my pussy, and Zed must have played some sort of prehistoric sport that required really good coordination. Zed's fingers were still working my clit, but like how they were when he finally wanted me to come our night together. He was also doing a damn fine job giving my ass a good fuck.

I came like a semi-truck whose break line had been cut, and it was headed straight for a wall. I crashed through the wall and destroyed everything around me. I let out a shriek an orgasm strong enough to bring the damned apocalypse back ripped through me. This time, Bash and Zed could feel it too and came with me.

Zed bit my shoulder when he came, and Bash threw back his head and let out this loud roar. They both thrusted out their orgasms, then collapsed on me. Bash got the giggles again. Bash seemed to get the giggles a lot. He had this deep, sexy laugh and it always made me smile. I didn't ask because he always told me what he found funny.

"You're right, Tabitha. If we did this before we stopped Drake and Mattan, the whole damned world would have ended because we never let you leave the bed."

Zed started laughing too. Zed had a nice laugh too. "Now that it's done, we can just stay in bed all the time. Tabby told me about this wonderful new modern invention where you can have food brought to you. I believe Tabitha promised to show me some modern-day human food we can't get in the kitchen here."

My entire body was singing. I was never a snuggler, but I loved just being held by Zed and Bash joking around. "Zed, I think we need to get you some Taco Bell. You can get a taco made from Doritos. It's totally disgusting, but I think that's right up your alley."

"I've got no idea what a Dorito is, but if you think I'll like it, I probably will."

"There's no Doritos in Heaven?" I asked. "What kind of Heaven are you living in if there's no Doritos or Taco Bells?"

Chase cleared his throat. "Are you seriously going to talk about Heaven food and Zed's disgusting food habits or are we going to get on with Tabitha's big fantasy?"

Chase never did like being asked to wait. I still hadn't had sex with Chase yet, and Gideon was like some sex god. He never came while I was riding him and playing with the others. I was going to have fun playing with Chase and Gideon, either separately or together.

"So, Conquest, how did you want to play this?"

CHAPTER 35

Chase just shot me this evil grin that being fucked by Conquest was going to be better than anything I'd ever had before. I didn't think Chase had any intention of sharing. He went all bossy pants and stood at the edge of the bed with his hands on his hips giving orders. That normally would have been a huge turn-off, but Chase managed to pull it off. Chase was barking orders like the General of a sex army, and they were going to conquer my bed. Bossy Chase was sexy.

"You two, out the bed. If Tabby is up for it when I'm done with her, we can all play again. Tabitha, I want you on all fours on the edge of the bed. Gideon, into position."

Oh, so the Horseman of Conquest was in a sharing mood. I didn't peg him for doing anything other than just him and me. I crawled to the edge of the bed, and Chase just frowned. He ordered me to face the other way. Now I understood what all Chase's orders meant.

Chase finally joined me in bed. I felt his hand caressing my ass, and then he gave it a hard spank. "You've got a beautiful ass, Tabby. I might go there later tonight if you're up for it, but not right now. I want to watch you suck Gideon off while I fuck you."

Kinky fuck was full of surprises tonight. Gideon slowly walked to the foot of the bed like some ginger panther. I felt Chase rubbing his cock down my slit. Chase just dove right in when I took the head of Gideon's cock in my mouth. Chase watching Gideon and Gideon watching Chase set both of them off.

Chase was slamming into my pussy, and Gideon was fucking my mouth. Chase decided to be bossy again, but it was an order I was happy to comply with.

"Finger your pussy, Tabby," Chase ordered.

My fingers immediately went to my clit. I rubbed it in time with Chase's thrusts, which were getting harder and harder. Chase slid a finger into my ass, and I was coming undone. I was moaning all over Gideon's dick. Chase was grunting and pounding my pussy.

"Yeah, suck that cock and finger your pussy, Tabitha. I can feel you enjoying it," Chase growled.

Chase had a totally filthy mouth. I could tell he was close. He had to be. No one could possibly fuck a girl this hard and this long without coming soon. My fingers were flying over my clit. Gideon's little noises of pleasure and Chase egging me on to suck his cock harder had my entire body on fire. I could feel from Chase he was close, but not Gideon. Gideon was enjoying himself a lot, but he wasn't ready to come just yet. Something was holding Chase back.

I started fingering myself harder and slamming myself back on his cock. Chase dug his free hand into my hip and gave my ass another spank.

"Come, Tabitha! Hurry!"

He wanted us to come together again. I focused on what he was feeling. I focused on the feeling of his cock slamming into me and Gideon fucking my mouth. Chase gave my ass another hard spank, and my world exploded again. Chase gave out this yell worthy of a Conquest fuck, and I turned into a pile of Jell-O on the bed.

"Oh, my lord, Chase, you can make a conquest of my pussy whenever you want," I moaned.

Chase collapsed over my back and started nuzzling my neck. "Am I going to get a boot up my ass if I ask you to take back that two-pump chump and the pity fuck comment?" I hesitated. I never took back an insult, even if Chase turned out to be a really good lay and nothing like what I accused him of the first day. I needed to be different with them. I needed to start apologizing for things.

I was just about to open my mouth to apologize, but Chase took my hesitation for me refusing. The next thing I knew, he had me pinned on my back and was tickling the mess out of me. I was shrieking and wheezing, but I wasn't fighting all that hard to get him to stop. I liked this. I liked cutting loose and playing with the Horseman of Conquest. I hardly got to play as a child. In addition to apologizing, I needed to start just playing more.

"Mercy! Mercy!" I shrieked. "You're definitely the Horseman of Conquest in bed."

Chase sat back looking triumphant. "I've never been with a woman I had something to prove before. You threw down that gauntlet the first day, and I've wanted to hear that from you this entire time."

"Chase, you don't have to prove anything to me," I said, kissing him gently. "I was just being mean that day, and all of you surprised me. I haven't exactly had the best luck with men, and I just assumed the four of you were like the men at the bar I worked at. It's something I need to work on. I've met so many good people in addition to the bad since I got here. I can't just assume the worst of everyone and go into insult mode because of my past."

Gideon was behind me rubbing my shoulders. "You had every right to insult us. We just appeared out of nowhere, and we *were* giving you a hard time. When we appeared, you had every right not to trust anyone and insult Chase. You have time to learn to trust people."

I whirled around. I also had time to discuss my fucked-up feelings and the twenty-six years it took me to get there. I'd been feeling like I needed to do this with the Horsemen since I realized my twin was the Antichrist.

"How have you not come yet? You've been inside me twice. Am I losing my mojo?"

Gideon chuckled. "It was hard, believe me. My tribe believed delaying your orgasm made sex more spiritual. We had totally different gods, but that was what we believed. It also makes it a lot more intense when it goes to happen. Ever since that night on the couch when you came without me touching you, I've wanted a repeat. I knew if I ever figured out what you were and it was actually possible, even if I died, I wanted to die with you naked in my lap having sex that way."

"You were kind of mean to me, you know," I pointed out. "You accused me of being the Antichrist."

"Men have been the same ever since my time. I was trying to push you away and try to pretend I was figuring out what you were because it made it easier to ignore my feelings and attraction to you. At the time, we thought you were just the Lamb, and I was conflicted. It felt wrong to have feelings for the Lamb."

I dragged Gideon to the sofa we were on that first night and shoved him down on the seat. If it was going to be more intense for Gideon, then I was going to feel it too.

And he'd been putting it off all night. After he'd been fighting some inner war, I wanted to make Gideon feel good now that everything was going to be okay.

CHAPTER 36

I looked down at Gideon sprawled on the sofa with his erection just waiting for me to pounce on it. I'd always loved redheaded men, and I always thought the gingers were a little magical. Gideon *had* to have magical powers beyond just being a Horseman. I came in his lap without him touching me. I rode his cock like a madwoman, and he didn't come. He fucked my mouth like the Horseman of War, and he *still* hadn't come. Did he have an enchanted dick too?

Gideon threw back his head and laughed. "It takes practice, Tabitha. People do this even now with Tantric sex. We have time for me to teach you. Now, get your cute ass over here. I've been thinking about this for a long time. I was willing to die for it."

I didn't immediately climb in his lap. I wanted his cock in my mouth again. Gideon ate the cleanest out of everyone in the house. Jana had started stocking up on blueberries and cranberries because it was Gideon's favorite thing to snack on when he was working on his computer. I'd been in front of some rank dick before and gone running in the opposite direction, but all that fruit Gideon ate made his cock delicious and he just naturally smelled good.

And he was the one that said it would be better if we dragged this out. I wanted to see how long he could wait. I sat there on my knees in front of the sofa giving him the slowest blow job in history. I was enjoying it just as much as he seemed to be. I could do this until he finally asked for what he wanted. His hand on the back of my head got a little insistent, pushing me further down his cock. I grinned to myself. I'll hop on your dick as soon as you ask for it, Mister Horseman of War. I'd already come more times that I could keep track of tonight, and I needed a little break, or I'd explode.

Gideon never did anything without thinking it through a million different ways, and he never did anything with me without explaining everything first. So, I was a little shocked when he lifted me off the floor and onto his cock. I just sat there in his lap with his cock buried to the hilt inside me looking at him in confusion. He'd never done anything like this with me before. He always waited for me and explained himself. He never just took anything.

His green eyes had a little mischief behind him. "I said I delay, but I don't like mind games, Tabitha. You know I always try to tell you what you need to know, but I think you are trying to play games with War and I'm the master of games. Don't try to force anything from me." I met Gideon's eye. I should have known this about him. I admitted I needed a little break and that was part of my game. Gideon had already forgiven me and was kissing my neck. "Then you should have said so. Are you ready or do you need more time?"

He could wait even longer if I needed? I knew nothing about Tantric sex, but I was definitely going more towards enchanted dick. When that thing did go off, it was probably going to plaster me to the ceiling. It was also weird as hell having four people connected to you on such a deep level, and they could read your thoughts. I didn't hear theirs all the time because I hadn't figured out how that worked yet to listen in. But they were apparently devious little snoops now that they knew they could. Gideon just chuckled and started nibbling on my ear.

"I'll have to get you a book on Tantric sex. If you want to learn, it just takes practice and patience. Nothing is magic; it was just hard work. Though, I would rather have you riding my dick than explaining all of it right at this minute."

I started moving my hips in slow circles. Gideon's magic dick could have potential. "How long can you put it off before you can't anymore?"

"My personal best when I was human was twelve hours. Time is different in Heaven."

I felt a little flutter in my belly at the possibilities of that statement. My hips sped up. "You can have sex twelve hours straight without blowing your load?"

"I have to switch up positions, or I'll get a cramp. If you don't want to learn, but you just want me in your bed for twelve hours, you think about what that means. Not tonight, but in the future."

Gideon wanted me to be direct with him and not play games. "Are you ready to finish now or do you intend to keep me up all night?"

Gideon laughed and bit me. "Oh, I think all four of us are going to keep you up all night. I warned you we're immortal and you're still human. I told you time works differently in Heaven. I don't quite think you realized what you were asking for when you decided you wanted all of us, but I'm glad you did. It just feels right. I want to come with you this time, Tabitha. I want the little minx in my lap who made herself come without me having to lay a finger on her."

I groaned remembering that night — the feel of Gideon's cock through his pants and my thin shorts. I had the real thing tonight, and Gideon wasn't holding back like he was before. My orgasm that night was intense, even if I never took my clothes off. I knew recreating this with Gideon now was going to be something else. I kissed Gideon.

"Take a little this time, like you did when you pulled me into your lap. You have my permission."

"Are you sure? I don't want to be disrespectful."

I groaned. "Gideon, get a little disrespectful. Shock me. Make us come together and show me what you mean that delaying it makes it better. Let go a little."

Now that he had permission, I saw a totally different side of Gideon. He started nibbling on my collarbone, and his hands went around me to cup my ass. Now that I told him he could let go, he clutched my ass and started bouncing me on his cock. I just threw my head back and held on for dear life. Gideon was practically lifting me in the air with his bare hands, and his cock was plunged back into me when he would set me down again.

His mouth couldn't figure out where it wanted to be. He was kissing and biting my neck and collarbone and letting out little growls. I dug my nails into his shoulders and just enjoyed the ride. I never pegged Gideon for any of this. Apparently, he just needed permission.

I could feel something intense coming from Gideon, and I was feeding off it. It was building a fire in my belly that had the power to consume both of us, and I wondered if this is what he meant by making sex more spiritual. It was more than just being connected to Gideon or that he had finally stepped out of his little box. It felt like we were going to bring the house down with us when we finally came.

Gideon never seemed to tire. I guess one of the perks of having four immortal boyfriends. He seemed like he could just bounce me on his cock all night. His teeth clamped down on my earlobe hard enough to pinch.

"I'm ready," Gideon panted. "Let go with me, Tabitha. Focus on what you feel from me and my cock in you."

I felt like I was drowning in Gideon. A huge tidal wave hit me when our orgasms hit. Either Gideon was right, and I was feeling that from him because delaying your orgasm really did make it more intense or I was right all along and he had some kind of a magic dick.

I had Santa and fairy tales ruined for me at an early age. I may be totally wrong, but for now, I was just going to choose to believe Gideon had a magic dick.

CHAPTER 37

When I got my grand idea for a kinky fivesome, I wasn't even thinking about the fact that the Horsemen weren't exactly human or how it would play out. It played out better than any fantasy I'd had. The Horsemen never got tired, and they never needed a break. Our night only ended when *I* got tired and asked if we could finally sleep. I asked for a break because I thought if I had one more orgasm, I was literally going to die and not get to live out the human life that was promised to me. It got to the point I thought I might orgasm again if one of them even looked at me cross-eyed.

It was nice sleeping in bed with all four of them. I felt safe, and I'd never slept that well my entire life. I woke up before them. This was my first apocalypse free day to do what I wanted with. I had a family home, money, and a bunch of cars I had no idea how to drive. Really, I could do whatever I wanted. Right now, what I wanted was to watch the Horsemen sleep. Was that creepy? They looked so peaceful, and now they got to spend more time on Earth before they were recalled to Heaven. Did I make them happy? I wondered if they had wives they had been separated from for song long in their little private area of heaven when they agreed to become Horsemen.

They said in every life, when the Lamb was safe, they always fell in love, and it ended in disaster. They believed it was a curse, but they kept doing it. Were they so lonely as Horsemen that they sought out love every time even if they thought there was a curse and it would kill them? Would it always be like this for us and was it a solution for all our loneliness?

I didn't want to get out of bed just yet. I wanted to stay snuggled with my Horsemen. It felt safe here. Someone was knocking on my door. It was this insistent knock like I was needed. The Horsemen all leapt out of bed, and their weapons appeared. I just held up my hand and answered the door. It was Jana, but she looked concerned.

"Miss Tabitha? I know it's early, but Mrs. Odelia is here with the girls, and she didn't want to come back when you were awake. She seems upset about something."

I sprung into Heaven's weapon mode. Lizzie and Ariel were witnesses. Maybe they had seen something that the angel didn't mention. Maybe Drake and Mattan had a way out of hell. I didn't bother with flashy clothes. I'd already landed the Horsemen, and they could deal with me looking frumpy if the apocalypse wasn't over. I threw on a ratty pair of sweatpants and a tank top and went barreling downstairs. The Horsemen weren't far behind me.

Odelia was sitting at the breakfast table with Lizzie and Ariel. Odelia looked furious, but I knew that look from Lizzie. Lizzie looked pretty damned proud of herself, and Ariel had the exact same look. I already knew whatever had happened, I was going to be siding with Lizzie and Ariel.

Gideon seemed the best at calming Odelia. He walked over and put his arm around her. "What is it?"

"Ariel just couldn't accept the apocalypse was over. She's gone too far this time!" Odelia yelled. "I'm grounding her for the rest of her life."

I didn't talk because I thought if I did, I was going to end up high fiving the runt and Odelia was going to ground me too. Lizzie looked like she was about to explode, but wasn't saying anything because her mother was already pissed off. I had a feeling whatever Ariel did, Lizzie was a part of it. Odelia had her hands full with those two.

"What exactly happened?" Chase asked, his brow furrowing.

"My seventeen-year-old child found out the true identity of the man Drake was trying to contact to be his false prophet. She's also managed to find out the identity of every person on those

Incel boards. She's doxxed every single one of them. I think every person on the planet knows their real names now!"

"Good," Chase laughed, ruffling Ariel's hair. "Now maybe someone will do something before they start committing acts of domestic terrorism."

"Can just *one* of you support me on this? I don't want Ariel or Lizzie poking Incels. It's going to put a huge target on their backs."

Lizzie snorted and then totally lost it. "They are Incels because they are mad no one is poking them. If someone were actually poking them in the first place, Inceldom wouldn't be a thing."

I tried to hold it in, I swear. When I started laughing, it set the Horsemen off. Even Gideon, who tried so hard to calm Odelia down when she was angry with her children was wheezing. Odelia was looking at all of us like she didn't know who she wanted to strangle first.

I was shocked when Odelia started laughing with us. "I should feel sorry for these misguided children, not make fun of them with you. Ariel, you did go too far. What if they target you?"

"I wrote a program to mass release the names. It can't be traced, and no one will ever link me to the leak. You seem to be forgetting those misguided children think *you* are a slut for having children and would have helped Drake take over the new Heaven and Earth. They aren't just harmless men posting from behind computers. They hurt people too. I did the world a favor."

"Can you just promise me now that the apocalypse is over you just be a normal teenager? No more doxing Incels and no more chatting with men with creepy fetishes. Why can't you and your sister just do normal things like shopping?" Odelia said.

"I was going to tell you, but you got mad at us about the leak," Lizzie said. "I want Tabby to know too. Ariel is helping me research how to start my own clothing line. I showed her my sketches from the clothes I intended to make for me, and she thinks I could start my own business."

I'd been telling Lizzie that for years, but we both knew it would never happen without money. Lizzie had that now and a mad genius sister to help her get started. I got up and threw my arms around Ariel. The kid probably thought I was weird as hell and she hardly knew me, but I owed her for everything she had done.

"Kid, promise me when you get out of college, you run for president or work for the NSA or something. You're going to do great things."

Ariel turned purple and bowed her head. I didn't mean to make her uncomfortable. Lizzie let a few more things slip because the entire room had gone silent now that I made shit weird with the runt.

"Now that Drake and Mattan are gone, all the powers we had as witnesses are gone. I can't blow fire or smoke anymore."

"Well, I want both of you to have normal lives," Odelia said, hugging Lizzie.

Lizzie sniffed. "I can live a normal life with superpowers. Dragon breath is way more effective than mace, and I was working on how to blow *I love you* in smoke to impress Natalia."

Bash put his huge hand over Lizzie's. "Then you're going to have to find another way to tell her that's just as impressive. Come on, everyone. The apocalypse is over. Ariel brought down some Incels, and Lizzie is in love. Why are we looking for drama?"

"Because it's weird not having something to fight for. It's always been food and money, creepers, or making rent. Then we get here, and it's the apocalypse. What am I supposed to do when I don't have to worry about all that?" Lizzie asked.

Odelia's eyes watered. "You just learn to be happy. You too, Tabby. You just focus on living now. Lizzie, you have your clothing line, and you and Natalia are adorable together. Just be happy. Please?"

I had the same dilemma. I didn't know how to be happy, but I thought I knew how to start after last night. The Horsemen could show me. Lizzie was on the right track too, and she just couldn't see it.

"Your mother is right, Lizzie. I'll be here to help. We can both help each other, like always."

"I think you got some feelings on you, Tabby," Lizzie drawled.

"Are they infecting like cooties?" I asked, grinning at her.

"Yeah, I think I'm catching your feelings. I thought we always agreed on no feelings?"

"Since we all have the feels, we decided on your new nickname, Tabby," Zed grinned.

"If it's Sugar Tits or Sweetheart, I'm going to be upset. I'm a weapon now, remember? I need a badass name. Don't forget my boot up your ass."

"You seem to have forgotten your boots today. We've decided you're the fifth Horseman. The secret Horseman no one has written about. You're going to be the Horseman of Retribution. Zed can make a room in hell and Bash can kill them to send them there. But you, Tabitha, you can blow someone to the Lake or a personal hell while they are still alive. You'll be able to do something none of us can do. You can send a beast of the apocalypse back to hell and you can use that power to stop the Antichrist," Chase said.

"Is Retribution a badass enough nickname for a badass girl?" Gideon said, smiling at me.

Retribution was actually perfect. I could be a vindictive little shit sometimes. I was going to have to rein that in if heaven was going to be my new boss. I was grinning like a total idiot at everyone in the room.

"I think she likes it," Bash said, elbowing Zed in the ribs.

"I could have told you that," Lizzie snorted. "Tabby is going to own that shit. Why didn't you consult the best friend for honorary nickname purposes?"

"Um, it was after Tabitha had gone to sleep."

"You finally got your fivesome?" Lizzie squealed. "I want details."

"Lizzie!" Odelia shrieked. "Not in front of your sister! All of you keep forgetting she's a minor."

"Mom, seriously, that ship has passed," Ariel said, rolling her eyes. "No one has said anything in front of me that hasn't been said by one of your stupid friends at a party or I've read about before."

"After watching my Oma get drunk and body surf at the party last night, really, anything could have been said in front of Ariel," I pointed out.

"The rest of you don't have to go out of your way to say anything further. I'm going to take Ariel home. I need to ground her for a little while because of what she did. Lizzie, dear, will you be home soon?"

"I'm going to hang out with Tabby for a while, and then I'll be home. Natalia and I are going to a movie tonight, so I'll be leaving after dinner."

Lizzie had changed. If we had been back in our foster home, that question would have been answered with sass and a lot of evasions instead of a legitimate answer. Lizzie said she didn't know if she could be happy, but she had already started. She'd bonded with Odelia and Ariel. She had Natalia too. Lizzie and I would always be close, but our little family had grown. Lizzie's family would be like my family, and I knew my grandparents adored Lizzie.

The Horsemen liked Lizzie. It was more than just her being a witness. They treated her like she was their sister too. I had no memories of my parents, and I sent my brother to the Lake of Fire. My birth father was a horrible person, but the people I pulled close to me once I ended up in Salem were my family. Only two of them were my blood, but it didn't matter.

I had my soul family, and I was bonded to the Horsemen on a deep level. All I had left to do from here was have a totally normal life before my destiny kicked in again and I waited to be called upon for the next time the Antichrist walked the Earth.

[Sign up for the mailing list for updates, freebies, and Arcs](#)

Other works

Literary/Psychological
Midnight's Sonata
Feet of Clay
Bette, Unscripted: A Dark Psychological Drama
Crow Girl
The Flight of Crow Girl

Paranormal/Science Fiction
Flash-A Death Story (The Usas Book 1)
The Usas Bellum Justum-The Just War (The Usas Book 2)
Lilith

Romance
Salome-A Modern Retelling
Fugitive (Misty)-A Contemporary Reverse Harem Series
Her Cop (Casey) A Contemporary Reverse Harem Series
Her Artist (Aiden)-A Contemporary Reverse Harem Series
Her Guard (Gareth)-A Contemporary Reverse Harem Series
The Sapphire Scythe (Aria)-The Order of the Red Shadow Book 1
Lethal Shadow-The Order of the Red Shadow Book 2
My Cat is the Antichrist

Humor
Attack of the Lesbian Farmers
So Your Cat is Trying to Kill You
Special Agent Mauve-Origins (Book 1)
Special Agent Mauve-Mission: Naughty Horace (Book 2)
Special Agent Mauve-Mission: Viper (Book 3)
The Neighbors-A Totally True Parody

Fantasy
The Spirus (Book 1)
The Spirus-Belisarus' Diary (Book 2)
The Spirus-The Lord's Uprising (Book 3)
The Spirus-The Gifted Child (Book 4)
Child of Fire, Child of Ice-A Sci-fi Romance (The Waljan Chronicles Book 1)
Escape to Ragnis Crystal (The Waljan Chronicles Book 2)
The Dysdaimon's Revenge (The Waljan Chronicles Book 3)
The Waljan Crucible (The Waljan Chronicles Book 4)
The Fall of Autrikxia (The Waljan Chronicles Book 5)

Coming Soon
The Rook Takes Their Queen-A Contemporary Reverse Harem Romance
Special Agent Mauve-Mission: Scorpion
Siren (Ship of the Damned)